AN EMBARRASSING DEATH

Bill Stemple sells secret photographs of the new Lanfair model to a French motor magazine simply as a foolish prank to annoy the directors of Lanfair Motors. As an employee in the publicity department of the company, he leaves almost everything to be desired. His outstanding virtue, albeit a negative one, is that he has not committed murder.

The morning after the office party a young female member of staff is found murdered. Bill had been with her the last time she was seen alive and had made a pass at her. He soon finds himself under suspicion, and under arrest.

There are surprises for all concerned in the legal proceedings that follow . . .

AN EMBARRASSING
DEATH

Roderic Jeffries

·BLACK·
DAGGER
·CRIME·

First published 1964
by
William Collins Sons & Co. Ltd

This edition 2006 by BBC Audiobooks Ltd
published by arrangement with
the author

ISBN 10: 1 4056 8538 7
ISBN 13: 978 1 405 68538 2

British Library Cataloguing in Publication Data available

Printed and bound in Great Britain by
Antony Rowe Ltd., Chippenham, Wiltshire

CHAPTER I

XXXXXXXXXXXXXXXXXXXXXXXXXXXXXXXXXXXXXXXXXXXXXXXXXXXX

THE BUS CAME to a stop in the car-park of The Eight
Nuns under an overhead sign, "Coaches by appointment only." The driver took a handkerchief from his
pocket and mopped his brow. Firms' outings were
always the same and if he returned the bus to the depot
in the condition in which he took it out, he would be
lucky.

"Thirty minutes only," he called out, "and not a
second more." He knew that at the end of the half
hour they would offer him a succession of drinks to
try to make him stay on and that he would accept
them.

The passengers left the bus in groups which were,
in the main, restricted to departments, Public Relations,
Advertising, Statistics, and the typing pool. There were
also two members from Printing and Dispatch who had
missed the second bus.

The saloon bar was already almost full and Bill
Stemple, from Public Relations, had to force a way
through the throng to reach the bar. He held up a pound
note and waved it. The nearest barmaid ignored him
and served a stout man whose face was prickled with
sweat.

Was there anything nearer hell on earth than a firm's
summer outing, thought Bill? Lloyd Llanfaider, founder
of Lanfair Ltd. and six other car companies and a man
apparently simple in the ways of the world, had decided
that his lads and lassies (as, almost unbelievably, he had
referred until his death in 1935 to those who worked for
him) needed a pick-me-up in the summer so he gave

5

them A Day Out At The Sea. He thought in terms of whelks and winkles, a ride on the Big Dipper, a healthy walk along the sea front, a dip in the briny, a wholesome (i.e. non-alcoholic) lunch, a period of complete rest during which people could contemplate the joys of working for an enlightened father-figure boss, and then the drive back after which there would be a quiet dispersal of refreshed and refurbished minds and bodies.

" Yes, dear ?"

Bill's mind returned to the present and he stared at the blonde barmaid whose eye shadow was running badly. " Two gins and tonics, two whiskies, and a Cinzano, please."

She began to pour out the drinks.

Lloyd Llanfaider had died in 1935, just as the church bells had been sounding for Easter Sunday. He probably died believing the bells had been rung to mark his death. What he had begun, continued. More acres of beautiful Kent countryside were covered by sprawling factory buildings, especially during the Second World War, thanks to several directors who knew where their loyalties lay in times of such stress.

Every year, there were the summer outings to Margate and only those workers who belonged to strong unions did not go on them.

" Two gins, two Scotch, and a Cinzano. Twelve and six, love," said the barmaid.

Bill handed her the pound note he had been holding in his right hand. As he waited for the change, he waved at Carthwright, an Australian from the same department. Carthwright removed his arm from about Janet's waist —Janet King was in Advertising and someone had once said that when she and Carthwright were together there was no need for captions—and pushed his way to the bar with the easy grace, but irresistible force, of a man who had regularly drunk in the Sydney pubs.

Bill handed three glasses to Carthwright, pocketed his change, and then carried the two remaining glasses over to their table at which Alex Wicheck sat between Janet and Sheila Jones. They raised their glasses and toasted their own misery.

" Where's George?" Bill asked Sheila.

She shrugged her shoulders.

" Another row?"

" Not exactly. But you know what he's like sometimes."

As he looked at her, he felt almost sorry for George. Sheila had the kind of beauty which sent a man's mind wandering, but she also possessed a firm determination which prevented that same man's hands following.

He drank. He had drunk a lot during the day, since there was no other way of surviving. He spoke to Sheila. " How about going dancing afterwards?"

She looked at him with her cool, deep blue eyes. " Where?"

He knew she could probably be tempted if he named somewhere expensive. Could he fiddle a further four pounds on the next expense sheet? " Let's give *El Toro* a try?"

" That would be terrific."

He wondered why he was taking her out? He came to a muddled conclusion that it was the challenge of her calmness. You knew she would never sit on your lap to take dictation, so you tried your damnedest to get her to do so.

" Bottoms up," said Carthwright loudly, and he drained his glass. He released his hand from Janet's. " Same again all round? Get on your feet, Alex, and give me a hand when I call. And whilst you're about it, you can order the next round." He pushed his way through to the bar.

Wicheck stood up. He was always ready to help

collect the drinks that someone else had paid for, but was reluctant to pay for any himself.

Janet spoke to Bill. " Are you two going out any-where when we get back?" she asked, in her dreamy voice which always seemed to be about to drift into silence.

" We're going to go to *El Toro*," said Sheila quickly. " Why don't you and Jim join up with us?"

" We're thinking of doing something else," she answered vaguely, and was not in the least upset when Wicheck laughed coarsely.

Carthwright called Wicheck over. They returned with the drinks.

About to sit down, Carthwright suddenly spoke. " My God, if that isn't enough to turn the whisky sour! Look at our elderly frustrated spinster having a good peer."

They all turned, looked through the window, and saw Corinne Hammer. There was an expression on her face which seemed to be one of disgust.

" She's like one of them Draculas," continued Carth-wright. " Turn you to stone by looking at you."

" Wasn't that a Gorgon?" asked Janet.

" Yeah? Well, what's in a name if the effect's the same? I've been wondering. D'you reckon she thinks like a human?" He sat down and put his arm round Janet's waist. " It's bad luck being given a face like hers, but hell, she doesn't have to take it out on us. Me and Janet were having a nice bit of cuddle on the beach and she comes along, stops, and says we were being nasty and giving the firm a bad name. What's it to her?"

" No fornicating on the beach," said Wicheck, in a voice which, although he had come to England from Poland at the age of five, was heavily accented.

" You keep your dirty mind out of it, Alex. Me and Janet weren't no more than having a cuddle and if a bloke can't do that at Manly, what the hell's the point of living?"

"Do you all?" asked Wicheck.

"What?"

"Fornicate on the beach at Manly, back home?"

"You got your mind into a rut when you learned the difference between the sexes and it's never climbed out. There are other things in life."

"Of course." Wicheck sounded uninterested.

Two members of Dispatch entered. They were not far from being drunk.

Bert Breslow, the larger of the two, spoke loudly. "So this is where all the bleeding nobs is." He was a paid-up and belligerent member of the Communist Party: no one with any sense ever made any complaints to Dispatch.

He came closer to the table. "You lot wouldn't be seen dead in the public bar, would you?"

"Not if you drunken bastards were there," replied Carthwright.

Bert suddenly grinned. "So you're still around, Aussie." He looked past Carthwright at Janet and studied her body in an unambiguous way. "You watch Aussie—'e's murder. Don't go sitting in the dark with 'im."

Janet giggled.

Bert pulled a free seat away from the next table. He tapped Janet's knee with a rigid forefinger and she winced. "'E's a right bleeder and no one ain't safe with 'im. The things I could tell."

"Go on!"

"Before you come, there was a bit of skirt . . ."

Bill lit a cigarette. The outing was following tradition.

CHAPTER II

xxxxxxxxxxxxxxxxxxxxxxxxxxxxxxxxxxxxxxxxxxxxxxx

WHEN BILL entered the kitchen for breakfast, his father had already eaten and returned outside. His mother was sitting down, reading *The Times*. She looked up. " Patricia is engaged."

" The bloke can't have been a very good runner." He sat down and stared at the toast in the rack. He had a hangover and wasn't very certain that he wanted to eat.

" Your egg is in the bottom oven. It'll be a bit tough by now, but I called you in plenty of time."

" I don't think . . ."

" Shall I get it, or will you?" she asked, as if he had not spoken.

He stood up and his head began to ache. He crossed to the Aga and used a cloth to take out the plate on which were fried bread, egg, and two rashers of bacon.

" You look as though it was a heavy night?" she said.

" The annual outing. Paddle in the briny, boys and girls, and give thanks to our Almighty Lloyd." As he sat down again he noticed she was looking worried. He and his parents seemed to be understanding each other less and less each year. Not that that was surprising. They had known a world of values, which about placed them with the Brontosaurus. In any case, nothing would ever make him understand how his father, after a first in Greats, had chosen to become a relatively unsuccessful farmer although he could have used influence and his own capabilities to enjoy a highly paid career.

" Mary telephoned last night, Bill."

He could imagine what Mary had said. " I'm sorry to trouble you, Mrs. Stemple, but I was wondering if Bill was there? He half said he would be round to-night." " No doubt you apologised successfully for me?"

" I said you weren't back. You're old enough, and ugly enough, to make your own apologies."

" She'll survive the disappointment."

" I would call it rudeness."

Mary was tall, a shade too thin, and had the kind of face that filled the magazines at Christmas time. It was impossible to imagine her doing anything that common manners or morals would not sanction. She was the only child of a man who owned and farmed two thousand acres east of Ashford and a further fifteen hundred on Romney Marsh. She would obviously make a wonderful wife, especially when her father died.

Margaret Stemple spoke again, in the tone of voice she had used from his childhood to tell him what to do. " I said you'd probably ring her this morning."

He nodded. Mary was the kind of girl to whom one felt obligated to telephone and apologise.

He ate slowly and eventually found some enjoyment in the food. He drank a cupful of coffee. Sheila had been very attractive and desirable, but mistress only of her own fate. If only she had been born the daughter of a man who owned 3,500 acres, instead of the daughter of a paint sprayer on the production lines of Lanfair Motors . . .

His father came into the kitchen from outside. " 'Morning, Bill. Good day down at the sea? Margaret, where the devil are we going to move that basic slag to? I thought we said the old barn, but that's full of broiler food."

" The old piggery, dear."

" Of course, that's it. My memory's deserting me. ' I sometimes dig for buttered rolls, Or set limed twigs for crabs.' Bill, Mary telephoned you last night."

" So Mother's just said."

"What held you? Too much bad beer?"

" A girl who wouldn't share her natural resources."

There was a short silence. Bill sighed. His remark, to be taken lightly, had obviously been taken seriously.

His father went from the kitchen into the hall, ducking under the huge, shaped beam across the centre of the kitchen roof.

" She's a nice girl," said Margaret Stemple, and then very obviously wished she had remained silent.

" That's her principal trouble," replied Bill.

: :

Bill drove the twelve miles to Corrington in his Lanfair Super de Luxe 1500. All senior employees were expected to drive Lanfair cars and to encourage them they were allowed to buy a new one every two years at cost price plus three per cent. The directors did not like to see a Hillman, Austin, Vauxhall, Ford, or Triumph, in the car parks. Volkswagen was, of course, a dirty word.

He reached Corrington cross-roads and turned off the A20. Half a mile farther on began the dreary rows of houses which Lloyd Llanfaider had had built in the early thirties for his workers. After a farther two miles, there were the factory buildings which somehow seemed to look even uglier than those of the Midland factories.

As he turned into the east gateway, the man on duty smiled at him. When he became P.R.O., that man would touch his cap. When he was appointed director of Publicity, with a seat on the management board, he would receive a full salute as he sat in the back of his chauffeur-driven Lanfair 5000. That was, if the 5000 continued in production. At the moment, it was hardly selling and Publicity had been told to jerk their collective fingers out. His suggestion for increasing sales to cigar-smoking directors had been a photograph of a near-naked model in the back seat, with the caption :

"How would you like to have this waiting for you after office hours?" Gurren had mournfully rejected the idea and ignored his, Bill's, retort that at least it was better than the original slogan of the firm when the cars had been called Lloyd Llanfaiders: "It's an L of a car."

He parked in front of the Publicity building. Two Lanfair 1500s, straight from the production lines, came along the factory road at well over sixty miles an hour on their way to the departure bays. Once they were in the bays, stickers would be affixed to the windscreens stressing the need of a maximum speed of forty-five for the first 1,000 miles.

He entered the building. Mrs. Berry, at the reception desk, looked up and ceased frowning for a moment. That meant she was in a good humour. He crossed the hall, with its elaborate floor of marble mosaic, and stood by the lift doors. Two typists from the typing pool came up, wished him a good morning, and began talking, in scandalous terms, about one of their friends.

At the third, and top, floor he left the lift and walked diagonally to the right. He passed the first open doorway and saw Oswald Parry look up. Frequently, Parry left his door open so that he could check up on what time the P.R. staff reported for work: but he never found the courage to censure those who were late or to report them to Michael P. Andover, the director of Publicity.

Bill went into his office and closed the door. He sat down behind the larger of the two desks and dismally wondered if the aspirins he had taken would ever have any effect. After a while, they did and he began to think about work. The visit of the Swiss German journalists was over and his next major task was to arrange for the coming of the Italians. They would be more amusing, but harder to keep happy. The Swiss Germans had been so conventional that the girls hardly earned their ten pounds, but the Italians were a different breed of men.

He looked through his mail. There was a thick brown envelope, with a London postmark, and he opened this first. Inside, was a letter and a thick bundle of one-pound notes.

He stared at the money in astonishment and then read the very brief letter.

> Dear Sir,
>   Kindly find enclosed the sum of two hundred pounds (£200) which our clients have asked us to forward to you in respect of payment for certain photographs.
>   Yours faithfully,

Good God, he thought.

He lit a cigarette. There was a sound from outside the door and, without thinking, he picked up the money and thrust it into his coat pocket. No one came in. He tore up the letter and stuffed the pieces into the envelope. When he had broken all the rules and taken the photographs of the new Lanfair 850, not due for its public début for several weeks and the subject of considerable speculation in the world's Press, he had not been motivated by any wish other than the rather senseless one of breaking the rules. Then, when the photographs had been developed, he had sent them to a French motoring magazine which always paid well for secret material. What he had really been looking forward to had been the commotion in the directors' offices that his action would cause, yet now he found himself two hundred pounds richer.

What an incredible fool he had been to give them his address at work. The stupidest man on the assembly-lines—and some of them were almost morons—would have known better than to do a thing like that. In his joy at the thought of the directors' fury, he had forgotten that their fury would be applied to the culprit, if found.

There was a knock on the door and Corinne Hammer entered the room. He could feel his face redden, as it had always reddened when he was caught doing something wrong.

She walked, with her awkward, lumpy gait, across to the front of his desk and stood there, glaring at him. Not for the first time, he wondered how her parents could have been so cruel as to call her Corinne? The name, Corinne, suggested a smooth, svelte woman with jet black hair and a pair of eyes which could crucify a man on his own desires : but Corinne suffered almost every major physical misfortune a woman of forty-three could suffer. Her body bulged where it shouldn't, didn't bulge where it should : her thick neck would not have disgraced a heavyweight wrestler : her jaw was rugged, to say the least : she grew a moustache : the only desire she would ever raise in a male would be the desire to laugh.

She spoke abruptly, in her harsh, unmusical voice. " You did it deliberately."

He touched the bulging pocket of his coat in which the two hundred pounds lay, without realising what he was doing. " Did what?"

" You did it to get him into trouble. It's no use denying it."

" Look, I . . ."

" Mr. Andover sent Mr. Parry a horrible message and I had to give it to him."

" If you could just take time off to . . ."

" You think no one knows what you're up to, but I do. You want Mr. Parry's job, that's what you're after. And you don't care what you do to him, a man you're not fit to talk to. You knew Mr. Andover had specially asked for that list."

"Are you talking about the line-footage we received last year in the Italian Press?"

"Of course," she answered contemptuously.

"I put it on Oswald's desk as requested."

"Oh, no, you didn't, and I know you didn't! You reckoned that if you forgot it, he'd never remember it because he's so much to do and think about and then there'd be a terrible row with Mr. Andover. That's just what you wanted, wasn't it?"

"Can you really think I'd plan to take over Oswald's job by putting him in old Andover's bad books?"

"Yes," she answered.

He laughed shortly. "If that wasn't completely stupid, I'd be flaming mad."

She stared straight at him.

"In any case, ought you to denigrate Oswald so severely? You're trying to say he's got a bad memory."

"It isn't very good and that's why he's always asking you to help him out. But all you do is to try to force him to make mistakes."

She was very much calmer as she turned and left the room.

He stared at the closed door. Oswald Parry was said to be a distant relation of the late Lloyd Llanfaider. Nothing else could explain how or why he had been given the job of P.R.O. He was shy, diffident, and uneasy in the company of foreigners. His ideas for promoting the sales of Lanfair cars could be put in a thimble and still leave room for a lot of water.

The inter-com buzzed and he pressed down one of the switches. "Stemple speaking."

"Bill, I can't find that list of line-footage for the Italians. I know you said you put it on my desk, but it seems to have vanished and Andover is screaming for it," said Parry.

"I've got one copy. I'll bring it in."

"Thanks a lot, Bill."

He switched off the inter-com and searched in the top right-hand drawer of his desk for the copy of the list.

Sheila entered the room. " Are you ready to dictate, Mr. Stemple?"

" Yes, Miss Jones," he replied, with exaggerated correctness, " just as soon as I've been into Mr. Parry's office. Sit down and cross your legs carefully."

She sat down on one of the wooden chairs and crossed her legs carefully.

" Did you enjoy last night, Sheila?" he asked, as he stood up and stepped clear of his desk.

" Very much, Bill."

" How's George? A bit sore?"

She pouted. " Sometimes George gets very angry with me, as if he thinks he's got the right to tell me what to do all the time."

Bill thought that George probably credited him with far too much progress. He left the room.

As usual, Parry was dressed exactly as a well-dressed Englishman should be.

Bill handed the list over. " Here you are."

" Thanks, Bill. I suppose the other copy got swept into the waste-paper basket and when it wasn't staring me in the face I clean forgot Mr. Andover was yelling for it. He's in a bit of a panic over the board meeting this afternoon. There's more trouble over the Lanfair Five Thousand programme."

" One of the research boys was telling me there may be a closure of production?"

Parry ran the palm of his hand over his neatly creamed brown hair. " Not just yet. We've called it our prestige car and if we suddenly stop producing it, it might cause unwelcome comment."

" I always said that was a ridiculous campaign. If you want prestige, you run around in a Rolls."

" You may be right, but we'll see. Anyway, Mr. Andover wants more articles about it sent off to the

B

Press. He suggests we concentrate on the fact that they're virtually hand-built vehicles."

"We've already done that."

"Give it a try, will you, Bill? Say that the factory floors were raided for men old enough to remember what a chassis looks like. Talk about the way each chassis is watertight. Isn't there an elderly woman who works on the leather and has been forty years with the firm?"

"So they say."

"Good, Bill. Put her in it and as soon as you like with the articles."

Bill left and returned to his own office. He went to his chair, after kissing Sheila on the back of her neck. He called the Press room on the intercom. Carthwright answered.

"A fifteen hundred word article on craftsmanship and the Five Thousand, James. Resurrect the old woman of ninety on the leather work."

"Hell, Bill, we've hammered all that so hard you can see through it."

"Hammer again." He switched off the inter-com. He studied Sheila. She dressed with a natural taste that suited her cool, calm, self-possession. He wondered if anything would make her less calm.

He began to dictate.

"A speech given by M. P. Andover, Esquire, at the fifteenth annual meeting of the Manufacturers' Association."

He walked across to the single window and looked out. To the right and left, the factory buildings spread out in an ugly desert of bricks and mortar, but immediately opposite there was still countryside. He could see sheep creep-feeding in one field, a herd of Jerseys in another, and the tops of a number of apple trees. It was when he compared the view ahead to that on either side that he sometimes began to understand why his father had chosen to farm, even if the financial rewards were never likely to be great.

He turned round. Sheila was regarding him in the quiet, uninquisitive way of hers which somehow suggested purity.

" Gentlemen. In the world of to-day, it is safe to say that the production of a first-class vehicle is not the finish of the manufacturer's job. He has to sell it. To a world that has come to expect . . ."

Expect what? That any one car really was better than the next?

He touched his coat pocket. He must bank the money at the first opportunity and so get rid of the evidence. How, he thought angrily, had he ever been so great a fool?

CHAPTER III

xxxxxxxxxxxxxxxxxxxxxxxxxxxxxxxxxxxxxxxxxxxxxxxxxx

LLOYD LLANFAIDER had been called, during his lifetime, a genius, a brilliant plagiarist, a leading producer of the obvious, and a typical middle-rutting Englishman. Only the description of him as an Englishman angered him.

He started building cars two years after the Rootes empire began and because he was essentially simple in mind but crooked in nature, he prospered. In the 1930's, the Lloyd Llanfaider 800 was nearly as popular as the Austin 7 : any similarity in their construction was bitterly denied by Lloyd Llanfaider, but not by Herbert Austin who tried to prove breach of patent. After the war, Lanfair cars (as they became after his death) fell to bits in overseas countries until it was learned that conditions varied, Lanfair tractors helped the groundnuts scheme on its way to total disaster, and Lanfair lorries were used with great success by the communist rebels in Malaya.

Lloyd Llanfaider had a social conscience in advance of the times. After he had made two million pounds, he publicly announced his debt to his workers by giving each department its great social outing to Margate and its great social dance. Happy lads and lassies made happy employees.

The dance for Publicity was always held on the Friday after the outing. As secretary of the social club, Carthwright spent far more on alcoholic refreshments than he should have done.

: :   : :

On Friday afternoon, Mavis Pollard wheeled the tea trolley out of the lift at twenty minutes past three. She served two typists with tea and chocolate éclairs and only smiled very briefly when they asked her how she was feeling. Except on the day of the outing, when she enjoyed herself with uninhibited gaiety, Mavis was quiet and retiring. The typists paid for the éclairs —the tea was free—as Sheila came out of one of the rooms and across to the trolley.

" Mr. Stemple's tea?" asked Mavis.

" Yes, please. And a couple of éclairs, please. He says he's hungry."

" They tell me it's not just éclairs he's hungry after," said one of the girls and giggled.

Sheila blushed.

" A proper John Don," said the second girl. They both disliked Sheila because it seemed to them that she was always trying to make out that her background was superior to theirs.

" Eclairs are sixpence each," said Mavis. " Three sugars, isn't it, love?"

Sheila paid for the éclairs and balanced them on the edge of the saucer. She went across to Bill's room.

Bill looked up from his desk as she entered. " Just in time to save my life." He gestured at the papers spread over his desk. " The Italians have come through on the Telex to postpone the visit for two weeks." He stood up and took the tea and éclairs from her. " Everything's got to be cancelled and then re-booked. I'll lay any odds you like that all possible theatres will be full for the new dates and all hotels bulging at the seams. Book me in to see the company's quack and call it nervous prostration. When the maharaja hears of the change . . ."

" Corinne was saying earlier that Mr. Parry had already told Mr. Andover."

" Then I'll bet she forced Oswald to break the news so that I didn't enter the picture. She suspects me of the grossest Machiavellian schemes aimed against her beloved Oswald."

Sheila did not smile.

He put the sugar into the tea. " I hope you're not silently agreeing with her warped ideas?"

" You're capable, Bill. There's something . . ." She did not try to finish the sentence.

" Hard and nasty about me?"

" I didn't say that. Mr. Parry's awfully nice."

" You don't want to be nice for this job—or for any other job, come to that. It's dog eat dog and the softest one gets eaten." He sipped the tea and found it still too hot. " Dancing with me to-night?"

" If George doesn't mind."

" George is a very kind-hearted sort of a bloke."

She turned and began to walk towards the door.

" Bring your tea in here," he said.

" I'm afraid I've rather a lot of work to do."

Before he could argue further, she left and closed the door behind her.

Bill leaned back in his chair. How seriously was he chasing her? From the time he began to work for

Lanfairs, he had decided to leave the typists alone —but Sheila had brought with her a calm beauty and a sense of goodness which had at first intrigued him and then challenged him. Pat White had made a point of telling him that Sheila was playing hard to get because she saw herself as Mrs. Stemple, wife of an executive. But then Pat would have slandered " La Gioconda."

He finished the éclairs, drank the tea, and lit a cigarette. It was time to forget Sheila and concentrate on the changed dates of the visit of the Italian journalists. Their visit to London, after looking round the factories, had to go smoothly or they might become vindictive. Last year, a large, loud-mouthed Swede had, through force of circumstances, been the only one of six to be given a hotel room without attached bathroom. He was the only man who wrote about the handbrake of the Lanfair 5000 which had pulled straight out of its mountings. His article had been entitled, " British Workmanship."

Gurren, in charge of advertising, looking his usual tired and dispirited self, came into the room. He crossed to the desk and stubbed out his thin home-made cigarette in the ash-tray. "Heard the latest?"

" I'll buy it."

Gurren sat down. " A photo of the Eight-Fifty has turned up in the French motoring Press. The directors are talking about bringing in a private detective to see who took it and flogged it to the Frogs."

Bill said nothing.

Gurren took a dirty rubber pouch from his pocket and began to roll a thin cigarette. " It came from someone in the firm." He licked the gummed edge of the cigarette paper.

" How can anyone be certain of that? There've been half a dozen Eight-Fifties going round the countryside on tests. Someone may have taken the photograph on the roads."

Gurren shook his head. He put the cigarette in his mouth, lit it, and a third of it dissolved into ash. " The background's clear and it's the research department. Someone's going to get booted out of the firm," he said, with mournful relish.

Bill stubbed out his cigarette. The sense of defiant bravado in which he had taken that photograph now seemed nothing more than childish stupidity. As for the money, had he known the reward would have been as high as two hundred pounds he would not, ironically, have ever sent the photograph.

Suppose they employed a private detective? Would he be able to discover who had sent the photograph? Obviously, yes, if the staff of the French magazine proved co-operative. Bill hoped most fervently that the French journalists would be as quick to defend the secrets of the source of their information as were English journalists.

He forced himself to listen to what Gurren was saying. The modern-day worker was disloyal by nature. In the old days, men felt a personal loyalty towards old Llanfaider. . . .

If only he had not, in his panicky hurry, already paid the money into his bank account. But then, of course, that would not really have altered anything. The photograph had been published.

: :   : :

Bill swore as his black bow tie twisted itself to a north-east south-west position. After vainly trying to get it to lie as it should, he finally decided to leave it to his mother to put right. He fixed the cummerbund round his waist and put on the dinner jacket, after which he studied his reflection in the wardrobe mirror. Sheila had inferred he was hard and unscrupulous— did he look it? He was handsome, in a rugged fashion, with a squarish face and a jaw which suggested a certain belligerence. His eyes were a deep blue and one girl had called them so romantic it made her feel weak : that had proved to be a lie.

He left his room and went down the short oak stair-case which, although it appeared to be old, was the only fake in the house. Everything else was original, or as near original as it could be after 400 years.

His parents were in the sitting-room, listening to the L.P. recording of Beethoven's eighth symphony that his father had bought in Ashford the previous market day.

" My tie refuses to lie straight," said Bill.

Margaret Stemple smiled and stood up. She undid the tie, and then with a few deft movements, re-tied it perfectly. She possessed the kind of quiet determined nature which ensured that most things acted for her as they should. " Are you taking Mary?" she asked, as she sat down.

He went across to the small oak gate-leg table on which were bottles of whisky, gin, sherry, tonics, a soda syphon, and several glasses. " This dance is for members of the firm only. If the men were allowed to take their own company, who would dance with the girls from the typing pool? For some of the poor dears, this is their one great chance of the year." He poured himself out a whisky and soda.

His father threw the stub of the cigarette he had been smoking into the iron fire-basket which stood under the canopy in the centre of the large ingle-nook fireplace. " They can't possibly possess as few charms as you always make out."

" Care to bet on it?" Bill raised his glass. " Cheers, and here's to a good hay harvest."

" Amen to that four times. I've held the cut back two weeks hoping for an extra few tons and now the blasted weather forecast talks about continuous light rain. The Almighty has a peculiar sense of humour when it comes to his dealings with farmers."

" I told you you ought to have cut last week."

" If I restricted myself to taking your advice, Bill, I'd be knocking on the door of the labour exchange inside a year. Remember advising me to concentrate on milk, four days before fourpence a gallon was knocked off the price?"

" Is it going to be a nice dance?" asked Margaret Stemple.

" Depends how you interpret ' nice '," answered Bill. " If it follows precedent, there'll be many a torn dress by the end. Even Tired Tim Gurren joined the band of happy lusters last year : they say that's what brought on his heart attack."

" Sometimes I wonder if these days people realise there are words with more than four letters," said Henry Stemple. He took a pipe from his pocket and began to fill it with tobacco. " If Kinsey had visited Lanfairs . . ."

" He'd have been shocked," cut in Bill. " But only by the complete lack of variety."

" In our day," said Margaret Stemple, " unmarried people were not quite so aware of the fact that there could be variety."

" That far back, mother dear, the gooseberry bush was still regarded with atavistic awe."

" At least it made the gooseberries taste sweeter."

Bill finished his drink. " I'd better be pushing."

His father turned round and looked at the gilt carriage clock which was on top of the small inset bookcase. " You're moving very early."

" Am I?"

" I seem to remember last year you didn't leave until nine-thirty and then it was to the accompaniment of groans at the thought of going."

" Maybe this year I'm setting an example."

" If so, I'd strongly suggest that no one else follows it."

Bill wished them good night and left. He went through the hall and into the garden, which was the responsibility of his mother and an old man who came twice a week. As always, and to very good effect, his mother had chosen simplicity so that there was a broad sweep of lawn, two large rose beds, a herbaceous border, and one small flower bed.

The garage was an old timbered cow barn with heavily sloped tiled roof which had become useless for its original purpose when a milking parlour, free of wood, was needed. It held three cars. A Vauxhall and a Land-Rover, both in need of cleaning, and his Lanfair Super de Luxe 1500 in red and light grey, which was in almost spotless condition. Members of the Publicity department whose cars were likely to be seen by the Press had their cars cleaned and polished by the firm.

He climbed in and started the engine. How was the evening going to go?

: :   : :

Sheila was dressed in a ballet length frock of red taffeta. Her black hair was set neatly and she wore a single string of pearls that looked good enough to be genuine.

George Willon, in charge of the photographic section of Advertising, sat on the corner bar stool. He rested his hands on hers. " Please," he said.

She sighed. " But I can't just say no to him if he asks me, George. That would be terribly rude."

" You can tell him I'm taking you to the dance, not him."

" But it isn't all formal."

" Maybe you'd rather dance with him?"

" Please don't start getting like that, George."

" What d'you expect me to do?" he asked sullenly. " He's always after you and you don't try to discourage him. What happened at the outing? He went off with you. And you went to dinner with him afterwards."

She drank some of the lager and tried to look as though she liked it. As she looked at him, she unhappily noticed how badly his suit fitted him.

"Where did he take you?" he asked.

"I've already told you once. *El Toro*."

"That must have cost him a fiver."

She had noticed that the bill had been over six pounds.

George removed his hand from hers. He finished his half pint of beer. "If you were with him now, you'd be drinking champagne cocktails."

"Please, George. . . ."

"He's got a posh car and plenty of extra money so he takes you out to all those expensive places. But I'll tell you something for free. He won't ever marry you. And d'you know why?"

She stepped down from the high stool. "Let's move, George."

Immediately, he became contrite. "Sheila, I'm only trying to say . . . Well, I . . . You know how I feel. It makes me all . . . all hurt inside when you go out with him." He flushed, as if embarrassed at having shown so much emotion. "Have another drink?"

She looked at her glass, still only half empty. "I don't want any more, thanks."

"Then have something else. Would you like a champagne cocktail, if they can make one?"

She shook her head. "No, thanks." But she moved back and sat down on the stool. "How was work to-day?"

"All right." George beckoned to the bartender, who decided not to notice. George hesitated, half-heartedly called out: "Another half of bitter, please."

He watched the bartender finally come over and serve him. He was certain that if he'd been drinking something pricier, the bartender would have been quicker

off the mark. It had been a mistake to come to this
pub which liked to think it catered for the " gentry "
of the district. He tried to forget the bartender and
answered Sheila's question. " Work's the same as usual.
I had to do two hundred copies of that new photo of
the Five Thousand for Tired Tim. They're starting a
fresh publicity drive."

" There was a conference about it."

" They're nice cars." Miserably and angrily, George
thought that only in their work could they find something neutral to discuss.

: :   : :

The band was at the far end of the conference room and
its standard of playing was no worse than usual. The
two chandeliers, last surviving relics of the days when
the building had been a dower house, had been switched
on and they provided a slight touch of luxury. On
one wall, with the special lighting on, hung the large
portrait of Lloyd Llanfaider, looking kind and bene-
volent.

The bar was in the next room, the conference annex.
Two of the firm's gatekeepers, glad to earn an extra
pound, served behind the trestle tables.

The heads of P.R.O., Advertising, Statistics, and
Printing and Dispatch, were expected to be present until
after supper, while Michael P. Andover and Charles
Janton, assistant director of Publicity, " looked in "
for ten minutes. Their arrival was resented and their
departure greeted with thankful relief. Senior executives
wore dinner jackets, except for the man in charge of
Printing and Dispatch.

Bill had his first dance with Sheila twenty-five minutes
after she had arrived. When the band stopped, he
suggested a drink and, as they walked to the annex,
they passed George, sitting in the corner of the room
and being talked to by Anne McCarren who looked as
though she was giving him some very earnest advice.

George stared appealingly at Sheila, but she ignored him.

There were many more people in the annex than on the dance floor and Bill left Sheila by the doorway. He pushed his way through to the trestle tables. The more sober of the two barmen served him.

As he was handed two glasses, a woman's voice came from his immediate right. " Having fun, Mr. Stemple?"

He turned and came face to face with Pat White. If her dress had revealed much more of her, Tired Tim would almost certainly have suffered another heart attack. It was small wonder that Alex Wicheck was with her. " Not yet," he answered, knowing that some such comment was expected from him. She giggled.

He returned to Sheila's side and handed her a glass. " Here's to us."

Janet and Carthwright came up to them.

" Have you tried the punch yet?" asked Carthwright. " If not, get cracking at the double. I got hold of some pure alcohol from a little nurse I know."

" You don't know any nurses," said Janet, and she bit the lobe of his right ear.

" Jesus!" he exclaimed. " That hurt." He rubbed his ear.

" It was only a love nibble."

" They still breed 'em tough in the Old Country," remarked Bill.

" If you ask me, they're breeding ruddy cannibals. You just wait," he said to Janet.

" I'm trying to," she answered.

Bill grinned. He was never quite certain whether their life really was as straightforwardly lustful as they made it out to be.

" Had a go at tombola yet?" asked Carthwright.

Bill shook his head. " I'm not supporting that. Not when twenty per cent of the takings go straight into your pocket."

"When I'm crooked, I'm subtle."

"He can be very subtle," murmured Janet.

"About what?"

Carthwright continued speaking. "I'm giving it to you straight, there's two bottles of champagne going. One of 'em was given by old Andover. Just stop and think what you can do to his gift after you've drunk it! Now come on, lay into the punch. I didn't make it for all the drunken bastards from Dispatch. It's strong enough to make your hair curl."

"If Bill's hair curls any more, he'll begin to look like a queer," said Janet.

Carthwright stared critically at Bill. "Part it down the middle, sport, and then knock twice on one of the director's doors after six. They say there isn't a quicker way of earning promotion."

"Now you're being nasty," said Janet. "You Colonials never know when to draw the line."

"Colonials! Jesus! We've been a dominion since before your father cursed himself for carelessness and don't you forget it. A great big autonomous bloody dominion." He smacked her shapely bottom.

She wriggled slightly. "That was nice."

Gurren, already somewhat unsteady, came across. He was wearing a dinner jacket that was obviously at least thirty years old. "Good party this. Very decent of 'em to give it to us. Makes for a happy family. As I said to Mr. Andover, there's nothing to beat a happy family."

"As you said to Mr. Andover." Carthwright's voice was filled with scorn. "How's your tongue? Sore?" He turned. "Come on, Janet, let's go for the punch. My little nurse said that that alcohol . . ." He gave a sharp cry of pain as his ear was bitten for the second time. He whispered something to Janet which made her smack him lightly on the cheek, then they left.

Gurren spoke bitterly. "They're disgusting. If they must be like that, why can't they keep it hidden?" He sounded both outraged and jealous. When he received no answer, he stared at Sheila for a few seconds, then he emptied his glass and left them.

Oswald Parry entered the annex and looked round. He began to walk towards Bill. Corinne, dressed in a full length evening gown that was far too smart for the occasion and her, hurried up to him. He greeted her, but kept on walking.

" 'Evening, Bill. 'Evening, Miss Jones," he said. "Warm to-night." He took a handkerchief from his pocket and mopped his brow. There was nothing he hated more than a social event.

" The forecast said it would be hot, Mr. Parry," said Corinne.

" And how right they are, Miss Hammer. Enjoying yourself dancing?" As soon as he had spoken, it was clear that he knew his question had been a ridiculous one. No one would ask Corinne to dance. No one could understand why she suffered the annual humiliation of turning up and rediscovering this fact.

Conversation began, stopped, began again. Bill asked everyone what he or she would like to drink. Sheila said another whisky, Corinne stubbornly refused anything although she was thirsty, and Parry said he thought he could manage a gin and tonic.

Corinne spoke as soon as Bill had brought the drinks to them. " I asked you to put the list on Mr. Parry's table, didn't I?"

" And I complied." He handed a glass to Sheila.

" You did not."

" Now, now," said Parry. " No shop out of office hours. Not on this night of all nights."

" Mr. Stemple's just admitted he knew."

" Miss Hammer seems to think I didn't put it there

on purpose," said Bill. " Always excusing the Irishism."

Parry became flustered. " I'm sure she doesn't really think that."

" Yes, I do," she said, in a shrill voice.

There was a short silence which Sheila broke. " I must disappear." She handed her glass to Bill. " Shan't be long." She went past two young Mods from Dispatch and skilfully avoided their clutching hands.

" You don't want to trust everyone so, Mr. Parry," said Corinne, in a sniffy voice. " There are too many people trying to take advantage of you." With an abrupt, ungraceful movement she turned and walked away.

Parry fiddled with his bow tie, smoothed down his smooth hair, and finally decided he must say something. " An odd woman."

" You can say that again with more emphasis."

" Still, she's a very efficient secretary."

" Maybe." Bill shrugged his shoulders. " How about the other half?"

" Not for me, thanks, Bill. I must have a clear head for to-morrow for the extra conference they've called. Saturday working, no less!" Parry lowered his voice. " They still can't decide what to do about the five thousand."

" Scrap it."

" Only as a last resort, even though we're losing money on every model sold." He put his hand in his right trouser pocket and jingled a bunch of keys. " I mustn't spoil your pleasures. Perhaps I could leave now and just slip away unannounced, even if it is a bit early."

Bill watched Parry leave. Sheila returned and he handed her her glass. " Drink up and I'll refill it then we'll go and see if we can win one of those bottles of champagne."

George entered the annex. He saw them, stopped, then came on again. His ill-fitting coat had settled down over his shoulders to such an extent that it looked as if he was wearing someone else's clothes. "How about a dance, Sheila?" he asked.

"I'm sorry, George, but we're just going to have a go at tombola."

His expression became one of pleading. "I've had a word with Reg and he says he'll drive us both home at the end."

She shook her head. "There's no need to bother. I've got transport."

George stared at Bill with open hate, then he turned on his heels and walked across to the bar.

"Poor George," she said quietly.

CHAPTER IV

✕✕✕

BILL BOUGHT five tombola tickets and one of them won a bottle of champagne. He and Sheila drank it during supper.

He took their plates back to the serving tables and then returned to where they had sat. He stared down at Sheila. Although she claimed there was not a drop of Irish blood in her, she looked Irish with her lovely cream-fresh complexion, softly rounded face, eyes blue enough to tempt the devil, and black hair. She smiled at him and then leaned over to rub the arch of her right foot. The front of her dress, cut squarely, fell forward.

"Shall we move?" he suggested, and his voice was thick.

"Back to the dance?" She sat upright and obviously had no doubts about where he had been looking.

He shook his head.

C

She moistened her lips with her tongue.

He held out his right hand and she took hold of it. After he had pulled her to her feet, he put his arm round her waist. He wondered how affected she was by what she had drunk.

"Where are we going?" she asked.

"Somewhere quiet."

He stepped forward towards the door into the passage and she moved with him. His left hand felt the sway of her flesh beneath the dress.

They went into the corridor. To their left was the reception hall, to their right a large room used to store files: ahead of them was the door which gave access to the basement rooms, most of which were occupied by Printing and Dispatch. He raised his left hand and again she made no move to stop him.

By now, he thought, most rooms would be occupied. So where to try? The basement door opened and, after a struggle, Janet and Carthwright came through the doorway together. Janet's hair was in disarray, most of her lipstick was missing, and there was a far-away look on her face: Carthwright was extremely hot, but not bothered. He drew Janet to him and kissed her ear. She closed her eyes.

"On your way down?" asked Carthwright. "Standing room only, except in the photographic department. Trust your Uncle James to know the good spots. Complete seclusion guaranteed and money back if no satisfaction."

Janet opened her eyes. "It's got such a comfortable couch." She closed her eyes again.

"And the best of Aussie luck to you," said Carthwright, as he held the door open for them with his free hand. "Remember our noble motto. We shall try the beaches, we shall try the ground, we shall try the fields and the streets, we shall try the hills: we shall always surrender." His voice was slightly slurred and he had difficulty in pronouncing one or two words.

Bill went to go through the doorway and for a brief second he felt Sheila strain against the pressure he was exerting on her waist, then she went forward with him. The door slammed shut behind them. They went down the stairs.

The passageway at the bottom ran the length of the building. It was only dimly lit and it smelled musty and damp.

They passed the first two doors and came to a halt by the third one on their right. Bill went in and switched on the light. She followed him. He shut the door and locked it. Then he put both hands round her, drew her to him, and kissed her with passion. She answered that passion.

After a while, he drew his mouth clear of hers in order to look round the room. At the same time, he explored with his hands to try to gauge the degree of resistance he would meet from her.

By the right of the door was the couch that Janet had praised so highly. On it was an old-fashioned camera tripod of wood and metal and he momentarily wondered why it was still there—surely they had had to take notice of something that big and clumsy? Around the walls hung photographs of early Lanfair cars, looking more and more hilariously archaic as the years receded. Immediately, behind him was the door leading into the dark-room.

He stepped clear of her, crossed to the couch, and picked up the tripod which he put on the small table against the far wall. " Coming to sit down?"

Once again, she hesitated, almost as if calculating her next move, then she did as he had suggested. She sat on the edge of the couch, with her feet dangling in the air an inch or so above the ground.

He sat down, put his right arm round her, and began to kiss her.

:: ::

Bill lit a cigarette. He threw the match on to the floor and stamped out the flame with childish petulance.

"Can I have one?" she asked.

He managed not to be so silly as to refuse her. When her cigarette was alight, she sat back on the couch until she could lean against the wall.

He smoked in silence. It had been an unequal battle from the word go. He had been exceedingly eager, she had been calm, apparently unaffected by drink, and perfectly clear in her own mind as to how far she would let him go. When he had reached that point, she had stopped him from going any further. Angrily, he remembered how she had whispered that she would allow no one to do "that" unless he were going to marry her. It had been a clear invitation to him to declare himself and it had almost succeeded. But since, in the end, it failed he could tell himself that he had not completely lost the battle.

Did she really think he would marry her, he wondered? It was obvious she considered him an attractive proposition and that, at least, was something for his ego to remember. She would have surrendered if he had offered her his position, his social standing, and his salary. Bill checked his illogical and hazy thoughts. Honesty reluctantly forced him to admit that what he was really searching for was a way in which to salve his own pride. No one could be happy at doing no better than George.

"You aren't angry, are you?" she asked quietly.

"Of course not."

"Come and talk to me, Bill." She patted the couch with her left hand.

He sat down by her side. They discussed a possible

picnic and then he looked at his watch. " Just after ten to twelve."

She yawned, as if the words had suddenly made her feel tired.

" I'll run you home afterwards?"

She shook her head. " There's no need to bother, thanks, Bill. I'm getting a lift."

The circumstances having been what they had, he was glad someone else was having the trouble of driving her home. " I suppose we'd better get back up top for the last few minutes."

She laughed pleasantly. " If you go up as you are, Bill, people will start thinking. Your hair looks as though you've just scratched it with barbed-wire."

He gave her a comb and she neatly parted his hair. He could smell the perfume she was wearing.

She returned his comb. " Let's go."

They went out into the passage. He turned off the light in the room they had just left.

" Isn't that George?" she said suddenly.

" Where?" he asked without interest, as he closed the door.

She pointed to the left, but the dimly lit corridor was empty.

" Maybe it was someone else, or just a shadow." She sighed. " Poor George." She squeezed his arm slightly.

They climbed the stairs. At the top, and when he was about to open the door into the corridor, she disengaged her right arm. " I've forgotten my handbag, Bill, I'll just slip back and get it. Don't wait. I'll be off immediately. I promised I'd leave at twelve, just like Cinderella."

He watched her go down the stairs. If she said it wasn't worth waiting, that was good enough for him. He went through to the corridor and then into the annex.

"Hey, Bill, come on over if you've the strength."

It was Carthwright who was calling him and he went across to the table at which Janet and Carthwright were sitting down and Gurren and Edward Vigen, from Public Relations, were standing. On the table was a half-empty bottle of whisky.

"I found that lying about," said Carthwright, with a grin and a wink as he pointed at the bottle. "Just as well, since the bar ran dry three-quarters of an hour ago." He lifted his glass and drained it. "Well, blokes, me and Janet ought to be moving."

"Where to?" asked Gurren, with a leer.

"You've a nasty mind, scout. Me and Janet wouldn't do nothing on our own we wouldn't do in front of you."

Janet giggled.

Carthwright stood up and Janet rose with him. "Don't leave anything in the bottle to go sour." They left.

"I could . . . manage another," said Gurren. He reached across for the bottle of whisky and finally managed to grasp it to pour himself out another drink. "He pinched this. Pinched it out of the funds." He added very little water to the whisky and then drank avidly.

From the conference room came the sounds of an old-fashioned waltz. A couple entered the annex and stared pointedly at the whisky, but when there was no offer of a drink, they left.

"It's been a good party," muttered Vigen, speaking slowly and carefully. "Enough to eat and plenty to drink."

"Not forgetting the girls," said Gurren.

"That's what really interests you, isn't it?" said Bill.

Gurren became annoyed. "I'm happily married. My wife and me . . ." He stopped speaking and drank. "I'll tell you something, Bill." He waved an uncertain finger in the air. "There's trouble coming for someone."

" There's always trouble."

" They've got a lead on the chap."

" What chap?"

" The one who took the photograph."

" What photograph?" asked Vigen.

" They reckon they know who it was," continued Gurren.

" Who what was?" asked Vigen, loudly and angrily.

Bill poured himself out a strong whisky. Was the drunken fool telling the truth, or had the liquor addled his brains? How could they have discovered anything? Surely to God the French editor had sufficient business morals not to reveal the source of the published photograph?

He finished the drink and poured himself another. He lit a cigarette. If the directors found out, he'd be thrown out of Lanfair Motors so quickly he wouldn't have time to collect his scattered thoughts. How the hell had he been so incredibly stupid?

He finished his second drink and poured out a third. Gurren was still trying to explain to Edward about the photograph, but his words were even more jumbled than his thoughts. Bill suddenly had to escape from Gurren's inane loquacity and he told the other two he was going outside. They took no notice of him as he left, glass in hand.

He walked out of the front door of the building and stood on the top stone step. He drank, and the whisky seemed to give his stomach a kick. Hurriedly, he lit a cigarette.

" So that's where all the bloody booze went, eh?"

He turned. Sufficient light came from inside for him to identify Bert Breslow.

" We pay 'alf a crown a week into the social fund, same as you, but when it comes to booze we don't get nothing. You bastards get the lot."

" I'll bet you haven't been depriving yourself," retorted Bill.

Bert was silent for several seconds. When he finally spoke, his voice was less belligerent. " Too bloody right, chum. I know these do's, so I brought some booze in me car. Come and 'ave some."

" I don't . . ."

" Maybe you is tarted up like a penguin, but that don't mean you can't come boozing in me car."

With a mind that was recording the sequence of events with some of the irrationality of a dream, Bill followed the other into the car-park and across to an ancient Hillman, which Bert Breslow had bought when told he was expected to drive a Lanfair.

They climbed into the back seat. After a short struggle, Bert Breslow pulled out a quart bottle of beer from a wooden case. He filled Bill's glass, miraculously not spilling any beer, then drank from the bottle.

Bill sipped the beer. It entered into open conflict with the whisky and the champagne and he hastily lowered the side window.

" Never met such a shower," said Bert Breslow suddenly. " I asked four skirts, one after the other, for a dance and not one of 'em would. Give me beer. Better'n any woman." He resumed drinking and the bottle gugged as air bubbles travelled up the remaining liquid.

Bill, staring at the building, saw that people were leaving. The annual social dance, given by the honourable and noble Lloyd Llanfaider, Dcd., was at an end. His guests had ceased to amuse themselves according to their various ways and now they were on their way home where, no doubt, many would find further pleasures.

" Crummy bunch," muttered Bert Breslow, as he temporarily removed the bottle from his lips. He belched loudly. "They don't want a man. Just some bloody little white-collared pimp." He resumed drinking.

Bill was glad to discover he was not the only man to have found the evening frustrating. He watched the people go. Two motor scooters went past, their popping exhausts filling the air with noise.

"I wouldn't lay any of them skirts if they begged me for it." Bert Breslow lowered the car window on his side and threw out the now empty bottle, which shattered on the concrete surface. "I've got me pride. Well, mate, it's me for 'ome."

Bill hurriedly left the car and Bert Breslow climbed over the seat into the front. The engine started on the third pull of the starter. As it left, Bill saw only one rear light was on and that was flickering. Or was it his eyes?

He put his glass down carefully on the ground so that it could be picked up by Mavis or her husband, then he promptly forgot it, swung his leg round, and knocked it over. More broken glass.

Walking with the strange determination of drunkenness, he went towards his car. To reach it, he had to pass an old Lanfair 1200, by the front door of which were two people locked in a tight embrace. He thought he recognised Janet and Carthwright.

"Good night," he called out. They gave no indication that they had heard him.

He sat down in the driving seat of his car and searched his pockets for the keys. Eventually, he found them. He switched on and started the engine, engaged first gear, and drove off with no more than a slight shudder to mark the faulty way in which he had released the clutch.

He began to talk to himself. I must not drive too fast. I have drunk too much and if I had any sense I wouldn't drive. But I must get home and anyway, because I know I'm affected, I'll drive calmly. I drive quite well when I'm drunk.

He reached the A20 and came to a halt. One car went past and then he turned left, in the direction of Ashford.

The road rose and fell, following the gentle undulations of a peaceful countryside that was marred only by a few cafés, garages, or ill-planned housing estates. He drove at what he thought was a steady forty and was astonished, when about to fork right at the junction with the Margate road, to discover the car's speed was over sixty. Hastily, he relaxed the pressure on the accelerator.

Did he travel on the back roads, or did he go through Ashford and then out on to the Canterbury road? At this time of night, when there was no other traffic, Ashford would be the quicker. At the roundabout, marking the by-pass, he chose the town road. He reached the tank—a memorial to the First World War which had, over so many years, lost any commemorative significance—slowed down for the double bend and was about to change into second when he saw a policeman waving at him from the pavement. Something went wrong with the gear change and there was a harsh mechanical noise from the gear-box. He cursed himself. Why did it have to happen in front of a policeman?

He braked to a halt by one of Knowles's show-windows. In the roof-mounted rear-view mirror, he saw the policeman stride forward. He told himself that he must keep his tongue steady.

There was a knock on the near-side front window. He leaned across the empty seat and wound down the window.

" Is something . . . wrong?" He could not prevent himself stumbling over that last word.

" Your sidelights aren't switched on," said the constable. There was a short pause. "Been out to a party, have you?"

: :   : :

Patrick Pollard, Mavis's husband, had been a paratrooper in the war. There was a photograph of him in battledress over the mantelpiece in the dining-room in their self-contained flat on the ground floor of the Publicity building. There was not now much resemblance between his two selves.

He left the flat at 9.20 and went into the entrance hall. From time to time, he pictured the building as it used to be and he imagined, with scant regard to period, women in crinolines and men in knee britches and shoulder-length wigs. To-day, there was too much mess everywhere to worry about anything but the time it would take him to clear it up.

He sighed. It had been a noisy party and neither he nor his wife had tried to sleep until it was over. She had spent the evening watching the television and he had spent much of it wishing he were younger.

He looked in the conference room and then the annex: both were exceedingly messy. They, on their own, would take a long time to clear up but bitter experience had taught him that this was only the beginning. He left the annex and went down the stairs to the basement. Anything could have happened down there and probably had. On one Saturday he had found a bottle of gin from which only a fifth had been missing. Probably, it was that memory which had brought him down to the basement so soon.

Within three minutes, he went into the photography room. There, he saw the body of a girl on the floor. Near her head lay an old camera tripod. Her skirt was folded back on itself and he could see that she had been wearing stockings but no pants.

CHAPTER V

BILL CLIMBED out of bed, crossed to the window, and looked out. No matter how much he had drunk the night before, how much his head throbbed, the view was one he could still appreciate. It spoke to him of the permanence of the land. Governments came and governments went, but the soil was always there. Seeds were planted, crops grew, they were harvested. Cattle were born and were reared, they produced, and the eternal rhythm of life continued. Straightacres Farm might one day be split into more than one farm, it might be swallowed up by a bigger and larger one, but the land would still be there, marked to the south by the sudden dip, to the west by the Aplington road, to the east by the copse which so often held a cock pheasant in winter, and the north by the Lea Hills. If only there had been as much money to be made from farming as from industry . . .

He stared down at the pond in which the goldfish lazily swam about just under the surface. The pond marked the excavation of clay, 400 years ago, necessary to make the bricks used in the house.

He slowly dressed, then walked across the small landing to the bathroom. Afterwards, he went down to the kitchen where they always had breakfast when *en famille*. His parents were both there. His father looked at him and smiled.

" Your breakfast is in the Aga," said his mother.

She had a theory that a good breakfast overcame any hangover and completely absorbed the remaining alcohol in the system.

44

He collected his fried egg, bacon, and fried bread, went back to the table and sat down.

" You drove over my mesembryanthemums," she observed tartly.

" I told you from the beginning that if you had that small bed so close to the garage nothing would live," said her husband.

" If people can't drive straight. . . ."

" Which your son and heir most certainly couldn't. I heard you, Bill, trying to climb the stairs last night. It reminded me of the labours of Sisyphus."

Bill used the salt and pepper mills. " I got picked up in Ashford."

" You what?"

" Got picked up by a suspicious constable."

Margaret Stemple's face expressed her sudden concern. " What happened?"

" I was showing a bit of what I'd drunk, thanks to a hairy ape from Dispatch. But I was perfectly capable of driving. I made the bad decision of coming through Ashford rather than trying the lanes and just as I got past the tank a uniformed constable imperiously waved me to a halt."

" Then you must have been driving badly."

" As I entered the town I switched off all my lights, instead of just the headlights. I tried to explain this to the bobby, but he got a noseful of whisky, beer, and champagne, and whipped me off to the police station. An inspector tried to book me for being drunk in charge."

" Only tried?" queried Henry Stemple.

" I smoked like a chimney, refused to say anything other than to demand to be examined by Cass and not the police doctor, and drew in deep breaths. The police doctor kept asking me what two and two made, but I didn't satisfy his curiosity until Cass turned up, cursing even more than usual. He called me a variety of names for getting him out of bed, told the inspector I was only fit for a chain-gang, and then declared me sober enough to drive even so inherently a dangerous vehicle as a Lanfair."

" And the police?"

" The inspector thought the police doctor ought to swear I was as tight as a tick when I'd been picked up, but it was no go. In the end, they released me after an embarrassing and very naïve lecture."

" Oh, Bill!" his mother muttered.

His father went to speak, and then stopped himself. Bill began to eat.

" It could have been terrible," she said.

" Look, it's all over and I've learned an important lesson. Never return home via Ashford : always choose the hills."

Henry Stemple took a pipe from his pocket and began to fill the bowl with tobacco. He wondered what the outcome would have been had Cass not been a friend of the family.

: :   : :

Detective Inspector Shute leaned his fifteen stone against the door jamb. He stared down at the body of the dead girl. " Are you sure she's Sheila Jones?"

Mavis Pollard nodded her head vigorously. " It's 'er all right. Shocking, ain't it?"

Because of his size, Shute tended to look lethargic, even indolent, and he had consciously cultivated this suggested character. As a result, witnesses who thought they were smart often treated him with contempt, which suited him because then they did not realise until too late that they were up against a clever man. " Look, Mrs. Pollard, you can give me a hand. On your way up top, ask the sergeant in uniform to come down and have a word with me, will you?"

Very reluctantly, Mavis turned away and made for the stairs.

Shute put his hands in his trousers' pockets and fiddled with some coins as he watched the detective constable take the last of the photographs. " Have a good look round for dabs."

" Yes, sir."

" Especially those tripod legs."

" Right, sir. Doesn't look as though her head was much bashed in, does it?"

" Hair that thick can hide a hell of a lot of damage."

The detective constable unscrewed the camera from the thin metal tripod he had been using. He put them both on the floor. " Poor devil. She got knocked off at the most exciting moment of a young girl's life."

The D.I. did not smile. The detective constable took the hint and was silent. He opened his battered leather case and took out a bottle of whitish powder, a camel's-hair brush, and a small pair of bellows. He knelt down and began carefully to brush the light-coloured powder over each of the heavy wooden legs of the ancient wooden and metal tripod.

There was the sound of footsteps from outside. A uniformed sergeant arrived in the doorway.

" Get on to H.Q.," said Shute. " Tell 'em that if it isn't homicide the girl was a contortionist. She's Sheila Jones and will they please send someone along to her home as I want one of the parents for a positive identification. If they can manage it within the next . . ." He looked at his watch. " Three-quarters of an hour, they'd better come here otherwise it'll be at the morgue."

" What about the address of the parents, sir?"

" The caretaker's wife will probably give it to you. She knows everything else."

As the sergeant turned and left, the detective constable spoke to Shute. " There are some clear prints here, sir." He pointed to one of the tripod's arms. " I'd guess at middle, third, and forefinger."

Shute took his hands out of his pockets and folded

them across his chest. It was very early days to feel worried by any aspect of the case, yet he was worried. When one found a girl who had almost certainly been killed by a blow and the girl's clothes were as they had been, one obviously thought in terms of rape. But he had examined, not too closely, of course, the girl's finger-nails and there was no skin or hair under them, nor as far as he could make out was there any bruising of her flesh. When a woman was about to be raped, she fought with the force of desperation and, generally, it was only then that she was knocked unconscious. If this girl had not been sexually assaulted, why were her pants not being worn? Why were the pants in the dark-room, neatly folded on the draining-board?

He walked forward and round the detective constable, who was getting ready to take photographs of the prints, and stepped over the girl. He refused to think about her too much because if he did he would imagine the last moments of her life and the terror she must have known.

He stood in the doorway of the dark-room. On the draining-board were the pants: on the chair was a handbag, belonging to the girl, in which was a plain envelope containing fifty pounds in one pound notes: on the floor, in the near right-hand corner, was a Zeiss Ikon camera which had almost certainly been dropped there.

What did the fifty pounds mean? Had the girl been a prostitute, or an enthusiastic amateur? He had put that question to Mrs. Pollard and had been informed in a very indignant manner that although there were several girls at Lanfairs who were certainly no better than their mothers, Miss Jones was nice, respectable, and always very polite. Had the girl's politeness to Mrs. Pollard been responsible for a biased assessment of character?

These were some of the questions to which it was far

too early to expect any answers, but Shute had worked out a system of crime investigation which had served him well over the years. Go to the scene, study it, and then start asking questions on the basis of the obvious. That fed into the mind various possibilities and from then on the mind always kept them in view so that it was consciously—and quite often subconsciously—engaged in checking facts against theories. This often produced truth.

There was a call from behind him. " The doctor, sir."

Shute turned. " Hallo, Doc."

Tyndan, a small man with all the traditional bounce and belligerence of small men, put his suitcase down on the floor. " You've not taken my advice, then?"

" What advice was that?"

" To lose at least a couple of stone. You're a walking hotbed for a couple of dozen heart diseases."

" Then give me thanks, not damnation. It's blokes like me keep you in a job."

Tyndan shook his head. He stared down at the girl. " Rape?"

Shute shrugged his shoulders. " I can't see any signs of a struggle."

" There's rape and rape. I'll take a few temperatures, make a quick check for obvious signs of injury, then pack her off down to the morgue for a p.m. You'll want a time of death, of course?"

" You've taken the words straight out of my mouth."

" I'll do the best I can."

" There was a staff dance here last night which started at around nine o'clock. She's wearing a dance dress so presumably she was killed during or after it. The last time the caretaker's wife saw her was at three in the afternoon when dishing out tea. I've sent for one of her parents so we should soon know a bit more about the times."

" Are you trying to do my job for me?" demanded

Tyndan, as he took from his suitcase an air temperature thermometer and a clinical thermometer with a range of ninety degrees.

"What's that, Doc?"

"I said, are you trying to tell *me* when she died?"

Shute grinned. "Needs a braver man."

Tyndan knelt by the side of the body and made a slow and careful examination. He tried to move the arms and legs. "Rigor's all but established throughout."

"Which means?"

"Twelve hours to come, twelve to stay, twelve to go. That's the first thing they teach you and damned inaccurate it is. Severe heat brings it on at once and gives the typical 'pugilistic attitude.' Did a case once where that cropped up and they tried to tell me the man had been dead at least twelve hours because he was so stiff."

"No doubt you corrected them?"

"Aye. I'll always correct people when they're wrong."

The doctor was a little bantam cock, thought Shute : a great deal of strutting, plenty of crowing, and unquenchable self-confidence.

He watched the doctor take the temperature of the body in two places, compare the readings, and then check on the temperature of the room.

"Was it warm last night?" muttered the doctor, as he took a second reading under the right arm.

Shute thought back. "Warmish."

"You wouldn't know what it was with all that fat insulating you."

Shute spoke to the detective constable, who had brought the Zeiss Ikon from out of the dark-room and was dusting it with aluminium powder. "You're skinny. What was it like last night?"

"Very warm, sir. I only had a sheet over me and even the wife stripped down to a sheet and a blanket. She's under an eiderdown at anything less than hot."

"How the devil does she expect the body to breathe, then?" snapped the doctor. "The covering should be the least possible compatible with comfort. An eiderdown in summer? Damned rubbish."

Detective Sergeant Rivers came into the room. He was a tall, thin, North countryman with the kind of face that was said to make women feel he needed mothering. "The father's arrived, sir."

Shute turned and walked over to the door. "How is he?"

"She was an only daughter."

"I know. Where have you put him?"

"Up top in the conference room. A constable's trying to organise some tea for him, sir."

"The panacea for all evils for the English." Shute sighed. Criminal death differed from natural death in that, being usually so much abrupter, its effects shocked more in the initial stages. Also, there were two sets of relatives to mourn: the relatives of the slayer as well as those of the slain.

He went up the stairs and through the doorway into the corridor. As he entered the conference room, a uniformed constable was offering a packet of cigarettes to a small, ferrety-featured man whose face had the pinched look of someone struggling to subdue grief. "My name's Shute, Mr. Jones. Detective Inspector Shute."

Jones nodded his head. When he tried to light the cigarette, his lips were trembling so much the cigarette jumped in and out of the flame of the match that the constable was holding for him.

"I'm very sorry we've had to bring you here to make the identification."

"It . . . I can't believe it's Sheila."

"Didn't it worry you when you found she hadn't returned home after the dance?"

Jones at last managed to light the cigarette. He

inhaled smoke with a desperate urgency. " She likes
. . . liked . . . to go back with the other girls sometimes."

" Can you tell me what kind of a dress she was
wearing for the dance?"

" It were green." He took the cigarette from his mouth
and nervously tapped away the little ash that had had
time to form. " That ain't right. She wore the red one.
Cost a fortune. I said she were daft to spend so much,
but she and the wife is always buying clothes."

" After you've had some tea, I'll ask you to come down
and make the identification."

" I . . . I don't reckon I can."

" Someone has to, Mr. Jones. You wouldn't rather
we asked the wife, would you?"

Pray God, thought Shute, that he was never asked
to identify the body of someone he loved.

CHAPTER VI

✕✕✕

HENRY STEMPLE bought Straightacres Farm when only
good land was worth thirty pounds an acre. Now, it
had to be very poor not to sell for well over a hundred.
The purchase of the land was one of the few good
investments he ever made and until he sold out he would
be unable to appreciate the benefit of it. He was rather
in the position of a gardener who did not possess green
fingers and who thus had to work twice as hard for
results less good. He had also always suffered from
a lack of capital. Instead of building new broiler houses,
he had had to convert two old sheds : mortalities among
the chickens were sufficient to reduce profit to the
break-even point or even to bring about a loss. When
he had geared half the farm production to milk, he

had wanted new milking parlour, concreted yard, and lying-in stalls, but he had been unable to afford the last two. He therefore had to employ too much labour.

Bill deliberately judged results solely as results. Because the farm had being doing badly, he had had to go to Christ's Hospital and not to Winchester, where his father had been at school. They had never owned anything but rather battered second-hand cars whereas some of his friends drove around in Bentleys and Rolls-Royces. For a long time, he had directly blamed his parents for this and it had only been after two or three years at Lanfair Motors that he had been able to understand how spiritual satisfaction could balance out worldly loss: yet, even then, he was by no means convinced that it should be allowed to do so. If his father had utilised his first-class brains, he could have made sufficient money at the beginning to have behind him now the capital he needed to farm.

Bill put the tractor into the lower set of gear ratios and then engaged first gear. The tractor moved smoothly forward, drawing the heavily laden trailer across the thirty-acre field. The sky was almost cloudless, but the forecast was still talking about rain. Everyone was working to try to bale and cart the hay before that rain arrived.

He braked the tractor to a halt at the edge of the field and climbed down to open the gate. As he returned to the tractor and drove through on to the road, he wondered whether to see if Sheila would come swimming with him on the next day, Sunday. Was it worth the effort?

: :   : :

Detective Constable Marrins tried not to watch the pathologist. He could usually mentally stonewall when it came to the more gruesome duties, but a post mortem always upset him. Perhaps it was because he always felt the proceedings to be sacrilegious as well as messy.

The Home Office pathologist stood up and stretched. He reached round to his back with his gloved right hand and rubbed. " I'm getting old and my bones are becoming more and more reluctant to bend. Very soon, it'll be the bath-chair and then oblivion, minus teeth and all the other things Shakespeare talked about. Eh, Marrins?"

" Yes, sir." Marrins was far too extrovert a character to have any respect for old age.

" Well, I've finished. And I record my utter surprise and astonishment."

" Is there something odd, sir?"

" How old was she?"

" A few months over twenty-one."

" Then underline this in your report. She was *virgo intacta*."

" She was a virgin?"

" I see you view the idea with the same astonishment as I do. Perhaps this day and age isn't as licentious as commentators would have us believe it."

" They thought she'd been messing around with a bloke. That's why I was astonished, sir."

The pathologist crossed to the small wash-basin. Marrins stood with his back to the girl on the marble slab.

" No messing around, no rape," said the pathologist. He began to wash his gloved hands.

" Then what . . ." Marrins became silent.

" The blow on the head also offers points of interest." The pathologist peeled off his gloves and washed his hands in fresh water then dried them on a towel. " I'll not confound you with a lot of long bastardised Latin names, but the girl had a very thin skull: abnormally thin. Because of this, the blow she received killed her instantly although normally it wouldn't have done very much more than knock her dizzy."

Marrins searched his pockets and found a rather

battered packet of Nelson cigarettes. He offered them to the other, who refused with several references to the dangers of smoking. " In effect, sir, you're saying that she wasn't meant to be murdered?"

" Young man, I'm saying no more than that she had a thin skull. That is where my job finishes and yours begins."

" How many blows?"

" I gather the weapon was probably an old-fashioned camera tripod?"

" That's our bet at the moment."

" Just the one blow, from behind and to the right."

" Would anyone know she had this thin skull?"

" She wouldn't know herself."

" Well, sir, I hope all this adds up to something that the D.I. can read."

" But it's Greek to you?"

" My headmaster repeatedly said I was dumb."

The pathologist smiled. The expression changed his face and made it obvious he was a man with a keen sense of humour. " Headmasters are notoriously bad judges and prognosticators of youthful characters."

" I wish you'd tell him that! By the way, sir, time of death?"

" I've done the best I can. I've taken internal temperatures and have tested the cerebro-spinal fluid, a test in which I have little faith since I've never found myself in sympathy with the originator of it. To my annoyance, both tests give approximately the same time : between eleven-thirty last night and one-thirty this morning."

" That agrees with the police doctor."

" Am I supposed to be humbly grateful that my small efforts have had the fortune to be blessed by the agreement of my professional brother?"

Marrins remained silent. After five years in the

police force, he had more or less learned not to let his red hair carry him into too much trouble.

: :   : :

Detective Inspector Shute put down the telephone receiver and sighed. His detective superintendent from H.Q. was coming down that afternoon for a report at first hand. What that really meant was that he would be complaining about all that had been done, complaining about all that had not been done, and pointing out how much more efficiently he, Easdale, would have organised the entire investigation.

Shute stood up, crossed to the window, and looked out along the High Street of Leamarsh. He was faced by an ungainly hotchpotch of old and new buildings, most of which exhibited all that was worst about British architecture. It was a pity the town had grown like that because so much of it enjoyed a wonderful view. On a clear day, one could see Ashford to the south and, beyond the town, the distant shore line of the Romney Marsh with the twin pimples that marked the atomic power station.

He turned. Before Easdale turned up, some effort must be made to tidy the room. Easdale believed that efficiency meant tidiness.

Sheila Jones had not been in any way sexually molested and the blow that had killed her would not normally have done so. Which added up to what?

The telephone rang. The call was to say that George Willon and Detective Sergeant Rivers were in the interview-room. Shute gave orders for them to come to his room.

They entered less than half a minute later. Shute held out his hand. He saw a young man, very nervous, who was clearly deeply distressed. "Thanks for coming along," he said, as he shook hands.

"I can't . . ." began George. He swallowed heavily. "I still can't believe it."

They never could, thought Shute sadly. Sudden death left everyone unprepared. " I'm sorry," he said formally, but kindly.

" Her father said she'd been . . . murdered."

" We can't be certain yet, Mr. Willon."

" But he told me her head had been smashed in and she'd been raped. Oh, God!" He gripped his lower lip between his teeth to stop it from trembling.

" Miss Jones was not raped. I hope it may help just a little to know that she was not interfered with in any way."

" Then why?"

" That's why I've asked for your help."

" But what can I tell you?" George ran the back of his hand across his forehead. " We were going out to-day down to New Romney and taking the miniature railway to Dungeness. And then, when I called at her house . . ." He shook his head.

" How friendly were you with her?"

George stared, almost defiantly, at the D.I. " I wanted to marry her. But I wasn't making enough."

" You thought you weren't?"

" She was too nice and good to live on the cheap."

Shute did not pursue that point. " You work as a photographer at Lanfairs, don't you?"

" Yes."

" You're in charge of the photography room and the dark-room?"

" Yes."

Shute was uncertain whether Willon realised the significance of that question. " Did you take her to the dance?"

" We met at a pub. I haven't got a car and that was one of the reasons why she . . ." He stopped.

Shute was convinced the other had suddenly realised he was criticising the dead. " What I want you to do,

Mr. Willon, is to tell me in your own time exactly what happened last night."

"I met her at eight o'clock at The Four Horsemen and then we went on to The Marlborough. We got to the dance not long after it started."

"Did you have many dances with her?"

"All of them, until Bill arrived." George's voice expressed his bitterness. "He's got a car."

"What Bill is this?"

"Stemple. He's in the P.R.O. department and has money to burn. I told Sheila it didn't mean a thing that he could take her to all the expensive places, but she couldn't understand. It's not as though her parents have ever been on relief: her father makes twenty quid a week, plus, on the lines. So why did money mean so much to her?" He flushed, realising how much he had said.

"Some people do like it rather a lot," said Shute quietly. "You were telling me about the dance."

"He came up and asked her and she went off with him."

"For the rest of the evening?"

"I went along later and asked for a dance, but it was no good. They went off to the tombola and of course he had to go and win a bottle of champagne."

"Any idea what the time would be for this?"

"I only know it was before supper was served." George noticed his cigarette, which had practically burned out in the ash-tray. He stubbed it out. "I saw them during supper. Afterwards, I looked for them and couldn't find them. James saw me looking and just laughed. He would. He said Bill had taken her down to . . . the photography room." His voice rose.

"James who?"

"Carthwright."

"Did you see her again?"

George shook his head. His face was white, his

features strained, and his lower lip was once again trembling.

" Have you any idea where Bill Stemple lives?" asked Shute, casually.

" Beyond Ashford, near a place called Aplington. His father's a big farmer," he said bitterly. Clearly, he believed Henry Stemple to be a very rich man.

Shute stood up and the chair creaked as it was released from his weight. " It's very kind of you to have come along, Mr. Willon. We're most grateful." He held out his hand and George automatically stood up and shook it. While they were still holding hands, Shute said: " Did you imagine Stemple was having an affair with her?" He felt the sudden start of the other.

" I don't know," George finally mumbled.

: :   : :

Marrins had arranged to take his wife over to his aunt's house to watch the Davis Cup match against the Italians on the television. Instead, he had been ordered to make certain inquiries. He had complained, whereupon Rivers had answered in so exaggerated an accent he had become almost incomprehensible: " If tha' missus don' laike it, tell 'er thee be workin' 'ard for promotion with tha tongue well oot."

Marrins climbed out of the police Lanfair 1500 (" We must support the home industries, however reluctant to do so experience has made us," the Chief Constable had said) and crossed the pavement. He knocked on the front door of number 26. The house was one of nine in a terrace and all of them badly needed redecorating. This part of Maidstone hardly fitted the description: " The second jewel in the golden crown of Kent."

The door was opened by a girl whose attractions were obvious. " Yes?" She stared past his right shoulder with simulated carelessness.

" I'm looking for Miss White."

" Then ain't you lucky."

" My name's Detective Constable Marrins."

Pat White's display of sophisticated indifference vanished. " What's up?"

" Haven't you heard?"

" Heard. Heard what? What's going on? Dad ain't in trouble again, is he?"

" Sheila Jones was found dead this morning."

"I never."

" She was in the photography room at Lanfairs. It looks as if someone bashed her head in."

" Gawd!"

" Can I come in?"

Silently, very shocked, she stepped to her left. He entered the hall and had immediately to avoid an enormous mahogany hat and coat stand. He bumped into her and this had the effect of restoring action to her.

" Better come in here. Me Mum's out at Granny's and Dad's somewhere else so there ain't no one but me."

He followed her into the sitting-room. A three-piece suite filled most of the available space and what was left was further restricted by the television set, a record player, a ragged pile of strip-cartoon magazines, a pouf, and a glass-fronted cupboard filled with china animals.

Marrins went behind the record player, was almost tripped by a trailing electrical lead, and stepped over the arm of the nearer arm-chair. He stood with his back to the fireplace. " You worked with Sheila Jones, didn't you?"

Pat White fiddled with the handle of the zip of the skin-tight jeans she was wearing. " We was both together in the typing pool and worked most for P.R.O. The other girls did Statistics and Advertising."

Marrins offered her a cigarette. " This must be a nasty shock for you?"

" You can underline that, you can. Twice over. Gawd! I still can't really believe it."

"They tell me she was such a nice girl."

Pat White sat down on the settee. "We always said as she was too nice. You know. Didn't laugh when we was telling jokes that was a bit blue. Seemed like they was too crude for her. Some said she was stuck-up."

"Was she friendly with any of the men on the staff?"

"She used to go out with George a lot. Welcome to him, she was. Not my cup of tea, I'll tell you that. Not with it; not with anything. See him trying to do the shake. Laugh!"

"Anyone else?"

"She made the running with Mr. Stemple. Wanted to be the wife of the future director of Publicity. I told her she was being a fool. He didn't want marriage: he was after something else."

"Weren't she and him together quite a bit during the dance?"

"Try separating 'em and you've had a job."

"Did they go off anywhere together?"

"Wasn't no use his hanging round the dance floor, was it?"

Marrins gained the impression that her main grudge was that William Stemple had never asked her to view his etchings.

   : :   : :

Detective Inspector Shute sat slumped in his office chair. He looked at his wrist-watch: nearly 7 p.m. Within the next five minutes, he must make up his mind whether to cease work for the day or ring his wife and tell her he would be pretty late home.

There was a perfunctory knock on the door and Marrins hurried in. "Guess what?" he said loudly.

Shute studied the round face of the other and noted the unusual signs of excitement. "Don't tell me Easdale is on his way back. A couple of hours this afternoon was quite enough to scorch my soul deeply."

" You'll remember the camera we found in the dark-room? You said to see if there was anything on the film inside and have it developed?"

" Well?"

Marrins took an envelope from his pocket and handed it to the detective inspector.

Shute drew several prints out of the envelope. When he saw the top one, he felt a sense of incredulity.

" Not quite what you send Aunt Agatha for her birth-day," said Marrins.

" Good God!" The D.I. looked through the photo-graphs. The position of the woman was almost the same in each of them.

" Feelthy postcards, effendi. Verry dirty, verry suit-able middle-aged Englishman."

Shute spread the photographs out in a rough semi-circle.

" Make ice-cold Englishman . . ."

" Shut that bloody nonsense up."

Marrins's leering smile vanished. For most of the time, his superior was, as a fat man should be, reasonably jolly: occasionally he wasn't and then he turned into a mean bastard.

Shute studied the photograph. " Notice anything?" he asked sharply.

Marrins thought of an answer, but wisely did not give it. " What exactly, sir?"

" You can't see her face in any of 'em." He looked up. " But it's Sheila Jones O.K. Comparison measurements will back that one up." He picked up a ruler in his right hand and began to smack it down on the palm of his left hand. " A pair of pants neatly folded in the dark-room. They make sense now. Fifty one-pound notes could make as much sense. This sort of thing pays big money." He leaned to his right, pulled open the top drawer and brought out the envelope that had been found in the handbag. " The superintendent's put the money in the safe, but being oncers they won't tell us much. This could, though." He looked inside the envelope. "First thing, check at her home to see if it came from there, then try Lanfairs. If both are negative, get on to H.Q., or, if it's too much for them, try London."

"It's odd, isn't it, sir?"

"Odd?" murmured Shute, as if talking to himself. "A nice ordinary girl lets herself be photographed like this. How in the hell do you begin to understand the human mind?"

"Looks as though Stemple didn't take her down to the photography room for the reason everyone thought."

Shute ran his right hand through his thinning hair. "If she got fifty quid for being photographed, the bloke who took them received his whack. We'd better take a look at Stemple's bank balance as soon as we can."

CHAPTER VII

xxxxxxxxxxxxxxxxxxxxxxxxxxxxxxxxxxxxxxxxxxxxxxx

BILL HAD FINISHED work on the farm at midday on Saturday and had then driven to the house of a friend of his who lived between Dover and St. Margaret's at Cliffe. He returned to Straightacres Farm late at night. As he walked from the garage, along the cinder path, to the back door he saw the light in the sitting-room. He was surprised, since normally his parents went to bed about 10 o'clock.

He opened the back door and stepped into the kitchen.

"Bill," his father called out.

"Just getting a drink," he replied. He took a glass tumbler out of the washing-up machine and filled it with milk, then went through to the sitting-room.

"Have you heard?" his father demanded.

"Heard what?"

Henry Stemple looked quickly at his wife. "It was on the one o'clock news and again at six."

"What was? Graham and I had a rush lunch and then took his yacht out."

"Sheila Jones has been killed."

Bill drank some of the milk. He felt shocked that death could come so abruptly, but this sense of shock was no greater because it had been she who had died. "The poor devil."

"Someone hit her on the head with a camera tripod."

"Are you saying she was murdered?" Bill's voice rose. Without thinking about what he was doing, he put the milk down on the small walnut pie-crust table his mother had bought in Ashford for fifteen shillings. "Have they any idea who?"

"Presumably, someone who works at Lanfairs."

"Why?"

"Because her body was found in the photography room of the Publicity building."

"Christ!" he muttered, really shocked now.

"Were you with her last night?" asked Margaret Stemple.

He stared at her. "You're not worrying about me, are you?"

"You knew her quite well," answered his father. "What's more, you went off to the dance like a rutting stag. You were with her last night, weren't you?"

Bill finally nodded his head.

"For long?"

"Quite . . . quite a time."

"I hope to God you didn't go near the photography room?"

"We went down there," he said hoarsely. He noticed the look of desperate worry on both his parents' faces.

" Look. It's nothing like that. We went down there for a bit, then we returned to the dance."

" Together? "

" Well, we . . . we left together. Then she said she'd forgotten her handbag and was going back for it. She told me not to bother to wait for her as someone else was taking her home."

Henry Stemple crossed the room and poured himself out a strong whisky.

" You haven't surely spent all day thinking I was mixed up with it? "

" No, of course not," replied his mother unconvincingly.

" I may have carried out a few manœuvres that wouldn't make a bishop smile, but I draw the line at smacking a woman over the head." He was silent for a few seconds. " Are they certain the murderer comes from Lanfairs? "

" What are the odds against its being anyone else? "

" Surely, it could have been? "

" We'll learn." Henry Stemple finished his drink. " The one thing that matters is that you're not in the picture."

Clearly, thought Bill, the police would question him. He would have to tell them he had taken Sheila down to the photography room, but with any luck that would be an end to it.

: :   : :

Gurren lived with his wife and unmarried daughter in a small detached house in a new housing estate. His wife was a hypochondriac who had destroyed the spirit first of her husband, then of the elder of her two daughters who had not had the sense or the courage to break free of the suffocating influence which ruined her life.

Detective Sergeant Rivers opened the small and over-

E

ornamented wrought-iron gate and almost hit Gurren on the head as he weeded the smaller of the two flower beds.

"Sorry," said Rivers. "I didn't see you there."

Gurren, looking almost shrunken in an open-necked shirt that was far too big for him, scrambled to his feet. "That's all right."

"I take it you're Mr. Gurren?"

"Yes."

"I'm from the Leamarsh police. One of the Ashford lads would have come along with me, but there's been a sudden panic."

"I suppose it's about that dreadful affair?"

"Yes. Sorry to break into your Sunday morning."

"But that's quite all right." Gurren was eager to help. "I'm only gardening and that can wait. Do come in."

They entered the house. They heard the sound of voices from upstairs, then a large and awkward woman, of about thirty, appeared on the landing. "Mother wants to know what's happening?" she said, in a dull and lifeless voice.

"Tell her it's just a friend of mine calling in for a moment, Brenda. I'll be with her soon."

"All right."

As Gurren and Rivers went into the sitting-room, Gurren said: "My wife's not feeling too bright to-day. It's the heavy weather. Would you have a drink? I've a little sherry."

"That sounds first class."

In a flurry of movement, which caused him to take twice as long as he needed to, Gurren brought a bottle of sherry and two glasses out of the inlaid mother-of-pearl cabinet and poured out two drinks.

"Cheers," said Rivers. Even to his uneducated palate, the sherry was raw. "You were at the dance?"

"I always attend the socials. It's up to the senior staff to set an example."

"Then can you put me in the picture about who Sheila Jones was with?"

"She was with George, first of all. A nice lad, who works for me."

"He was pretty keen on her, wasn't he?"

"Wanted to marry her."

"Someone said she didn't stay with him all evening."

Gurren's lined face had not expressed so much vivacity in years. "She went off with Bill Stemple. He just wouldn't leave her alone, I know that for a fact. Because he comes from a moneyed family, he thinks he can act as he likes. I can tell you a few stories about him." There was a pause, which was not broken by the detective. "The poor girl went out with him because he had a new car and took her to all the expensive restaurants."

"When was she with him on the night of the dance?"

"They had supper together and then disappeared."

"You saw them go?"

"Not quite." Gurren finished his sherry. "But I do know they were both missing for a long time."

"You must have some idea when they left?"

"I'd say it was around eleven." Gurren coughed. "It's disgusting, what goes on. It shouldn't be allowed."

Evidently, thought Rivers, a dance at Lanfairs was a very different kettle of fish from a police social. "Did you see them again after this?"

"Only him." Gurren lowered his voice. "I never saw her again."

"And how was he?"

"In a terrible state."

"What makes you say that?"

"I was having a drink with Edward Vigen, Janet King, and James Carthwright. He'd pinched . . .

Oh, dear, I shouldn't have said that . . . We were drinking whisky. Bill Stemple came along. He drank several whiskies as quickly as ever he could get them down his throat. If I've seen a man who was frightened, it was him."

" Maybe he always takes his liquor quickly?"

" It wasn't anything like normal drinking. Look, he couldn't keep his hands still and he was trembling all over. I suppose . . . he was remembering what happened down there and how he'd killed her after ravishing her."

Rivers was almost disgusted by Gurren's tone of voice. " Carthwright, Vigen, and Miss King were there. Have I got that right?"

" He was trembling so much . . ."

" Have you any idea where they live?" Rivers took a notebook out of his pocket.

" I can tell you where Carthwright lives, I think. He's bound to know where Miss King lives."

" Let's be having it then." After he had written down the address, he closed the notebook. He finished the sherry. " Did George Willon go out with her for a spot of hot hands during the evening?"

" He's too nice a lad to do that sort of thing. I say, let's have another little drink? I don't normally have two, but after what's happened I definitely feel I need something."

Rivers held out his glass. " Then as far as you know, Willon didn't leave the dance floor with her?"

" No." Gurren refilled the detective's glass.

" Did you see him at all towards the end of the dance?"

" He was around all the time, talking to Miss McCarren for most of it. Now there's a nice sensible woman who'd never go down to the basement." Gurren lowered his voice slightly. " What really happened to the girl down there?"

: :   : :

" Gurren?" said Carthwright, in his digs. He looked at the detective sergeant. " That bloody old fool was too tight to see anything but pink elephants. He instinctively knows when someone's opening a bottle. Plonk-pirates, we call 'em back home."

Rivers smiled. Carthwright's obvious character appealed to him. " Then did Stemple have these drinks Mr. Gurren says he did?"

" He had one, sure."

" More than one?"

" I wasn't checking. Hell, man, a couple of drinks doesn't mean anything."

" Who said they did?"

" You're not using up Sunday asking me questions just to amuse yourself."

" When he joined the four of you, would you say he drank quickly?"

Carthwright spoke uncertainly. " He maybe downed what he had smartly."

" You agree with Mr. Gurren and Mr. Vigen on that, then, even if you disagree on the other points?"

" Ted Vigen is one of those dreaming English bastards who tells you black's white and really believes it."

" You don't like him?"

" I like him plenty. But that doesn't stop me underlining a few of his imperfections."

::   ::

Corinne Hammer's flat immediately suggested the middle age of a fussy spinster, an impression gained from rose-patterned curtains, puce-coloured cornflowers on the wallpaper, a plethora of family photographs, and a mantelpiece thick with seaside souvenirs.

Detective Constable Marrins longed to open the windows wide. It all reminded him so much of an elderly cousin of his wife's. " Did you happen to notice them at supper, Miss Hammer?"

"I did. His behaviour made it difficult to avoid noticing him."

"Did you see them after supper?"

"When they left the room together, yes."

"And after that?"

"Mr. Stemple returned on his own."

"You're quite certain of that?"

"I wouldn't say so if I weren't."

"Can you say what he did when he came back?"

"I imagine he drank with all the others. They mostly do. They don't care what kind of a disgusting scene they make." She spoke shrilly. "One expects that kind of behaviour from an Australian, but not from a man in Mr. Gurren's position."

"They tell me he was so tight he couldn't even ask for another."

"I am not prepared to talk about it," she answered, with crushing pompousness.

"Was George Willon around?"

"Mr. Willon is a respectable young man who knows how to behave himself. I feel desperately sorry for him, but then a girl like Sheila Jones could not be expected to respect decency, especially when offered the example of Miss King. If I had my way, Miss King would . . ."

Marrins spoke hurriedly. "Did you see Willon at the end of the dance?"

"I don't know about at the end. I can tell you that he was talking to Miss McCarren for a great deal of the time."

Marrins thankfully decided he had asked all the questions the D.I. could imagine he should ask this dusty, frustrated woman.

: :   : :

The D.I. went from his office into the general room and from there to the superintendent's office. He knocked on the door and went in.

Superintendent Littlefield, in charge of U division, was a humourless man who would never have attained command of a division but for the deaths of two men at a time most favourable to his promotion chances.

"I thought you might like a run-down on what's been happening," said Shute. He crossed to the chair in front of the desk and sat down, not waiting to be asked. Littlefield had a habit of not asking his juniors to sit because that underlined his own position of authority.

"I expected a report before now," replied Littlefield, in his high-pitched, almost squeaky voice.

"The trouble is, sir, we've all been so busy."

"Superintendent Easdale phoned down from H.Q. He was annoyed to find you out."

"I've been making inquiries."

"He's coming down here first thing to-morrow morning."

Shute sighed.

"Well?" said Littlefield. "What's your report?"

"We've gone about as far as we can go for a Sunday, sir. The obvious suspects at the moment are Stemple or Willon, with my money on Stemple. But there's been precious little proof turned up."

"You told me you had a finger-print on the tripod."

"We've established it wasn't Willon's."

"Then was it Stemple's?"

"I haven't gone that far yet, sir."

"Why not?"

"Because I'd rather work in my own way. We've carried out several interviews and it's pretty certain Stemple took the girl down to the photography room. A man called Carthwright has admitted to suggesting to Stemple that he and the girl use that room."

"Sounds as though they were running a brothel."

"The youth of to-day having a little innocent fun. Anyway, the girl wasn't seen again from the time she went down to the basement with Stemple. When he came up top, it seems he was in a pretty agitated state. Drinking like a fish."

Littlefield searched amongst the papers on his desk and he at last picked out one. " I can't think why Stemple was released by the Ashford police when they found him drunk in the car."

They both knew that at the moment this had nothing to do with the case.

" What are you going to do now?" demanded Littlefield.

" Go home for a bath, sir. Otherwise, I'll have to offer my services to Amplex."

Littlefield was not amused.

: :   : :

Bill turned away from the television screen and saw the look on his mother's face. " It's not quite that bad," he said, in an attempt at humour.

His father stood up, a trifle stiffly because of so many hours on the tractor, and went across to the television set. He switched it off. " We're both worried sick," he said bluntly.

" Why?"

" Someone killed her."

" But it wasn't me."

" You were down there with her."

" And when I left her, she was very much alive. If I didn't do it, no one can begin to prove I did."

" It's not going to be very pleasant, is it, Bill?" said his mother. " Whatever happens, people are going to think the worst of your visit to that room."

" Then it'll be wishful thinking. For all the progress I made, she could have been wearing a chastity belt."

" Do you think you ought to talk like that?"

Bill stood up and crossed to the tray of drinks. He poured himself out the fifth whisky of the evening. " I'm giving you the plain, unvarnished truth." He turned round. "Surely to God you can't really think I killed her?"

They were silent.

"Someone did," Henry Stemple finally said.

CHAPTER VIII

xxxxxxxxxxxxxxxxxxxxxxxxxxxxxxxxxxxxxxxxxxxxxxxxxxxxxx

BILL ENTERED Publicity and said good morning to Mrs. Berry, who was knitting. She stared at him for several seconds before suddenly realising what she was doing. She hurriedly looked away.

"Can you let me have ten Oliviers?" he asked.

She used a small key to open one of the drawers of the desk. She searched amongst the packets of cigarettes. "I'm afraid there aren't any left."

"Then I'll take Nelsons."

She gave him a packet of ten and the change from half a crown. It seemed to him that she jerked her hand away so that there should be no physical contact between them.

He walked across to the lift. Pat White came up and stood by his side. "Good morning, Mr. Stemple," she said loudly.

He noticed that her hair badly needed re-peroxiding. "'Morning."

"How are you, Mr. Stemple?"

"Pretty much as I was Friday night."

She giggled.

The lift arrived and he opened the doors. He was about to close the doors when there was a call. Carthwright ran into the lift.

"Bloody alarm-clock never went off," said Carthwright puffing slightly. "Made in England, that was the trouble." He looked at Pat White. "What's with you, lovely, looking like a lost dream? Your dearest and best dropped down dead from overwork?"

She was embarrassed by the unfortunate choice of words. Carthwright grinned.

Bill was the last out at the third floor. As he walked across to his office, Corinne Hammer came from the opposite direction. She hesitated, then went past him in an ungainly rush. He continued into the office and sat behind his desk. It was odd, he thought bitterly, and knew he was being naïve, but this was the first time he had considered the possibility that people might think he had killed Sheila.

He opened the top letter in the post file. Spain wanted photographs and full details of the Lanfair 850, which had just been announced in the French Press. Was it front wheel drive, was the engine tilted, and did it have a special suspension?

Bill remembered the two hundred pounds.

He read through the rest of the mail. He flicked down the typing-pool switch of the inter-com.

"Ask Miss . . ." He stopped. Incredibly, he had been about to ask them to send Miss Jones up. He felt the sweat break out on his forehead.

"Yes?" said the distorted female voice.

"Send someone up to take three letters."

"Yes, Mr. Stemple."

He leaned back in his chair, took a handkerchief from his pocket, and wiped his brow.

: :   : :

The manager of Prentby & Sons, Ltd., London, was bald and he wore very heavily rimmed glasses which he was continually taking off and polishing with a small piece of wash leather.

"Kent have asked us to see if you can identify this envelope," said the detective constable, as he handed it across the desk.

The manager replaced his glasses, dropped the leather on to the desk and picked up the envelope. He held it up to the light. " It's certainly one of ours."

" Now for the sixty-four dollar question," said the detective, an elderly man who had once been a detective sergeant but who had questioned a suspected thug too harshly, too openly. " How far d'you reckon you can go in identifying it?"

" What exactly d'you mean?"

" Could you tell us in what part of the country this was sold?"

" Have you any idea how many envelopes a month we produce?"

" None."

" Just under a million. A year's production would reach to Scotland and back I don't know how many times."

" Oh! You don't think you'll be able to help us then, sir?"

The manager picked up the envelope again, examined each face carefully, after which he pressed in the two ends so that the middle ballooned out. He looked inside. " Any objection to me slitting it open?"

" I don't think so."

He used a bone-handled paper-knife and carefully opened out the envelope so that it became a rectangle with a triangle on one end and a V on the other. After studying it carefully, he looked up. " There's a fault. Too much gum which came squirting over the paper. Between you and me, this should never have left the factory."

" Can that help?"

" It might, if we can find which machine suffered from this fault. Then it'll depend on how long it was before anyone discovered it."

" We'd be very grateful, sir, if you could follow it up as far as possible."

" What's the trouble?"

" A pretty serious case."

" Oh, well, I'll do what I can. But no promises, mark you : none. You know as well as I do what the workers are these days. The fault may have been there all day and the machine operator was too damn' lazy to do anything; or else no records were kept."

: :   : :

Bill was called into Parry's office at midday. As he crossed the carpet, Parry nervously played with a ruler.

" Sit you down, Bill." He was silent until Bill was seated. " I've just suffered a long half hour with Mr. Andover."

" How is the maharaja?"

" Livery. Very distinctly livery."

The rate of the tapping of the ruler increased. After a while, Parry spoke again. " He was very rude."

" Over what? The murder?"

" That's roughly how it started." Parry put down the ruler. He folded his arms across his chest. Almost immediately, he unfolded them and reached out to pick up the ruler again. " He began by asking me if I'd seen all the terrible publicity the firm was getting. Had I read the Sunday papers? Had I read the scurrilous articles on Lloyd Llanfaider? Did I realise what they were saying about our founder? Finally, Mr. Andover went for me because the murder had been in my department." Parry's voice rose. " As I told him, the typing pool doesn't come under my jurisdiction and in any case, I can't hold myself responsible for a thing like this."

Bill could imagine Parry's aggrieved pomposity.

" Then, in his usual way, he began telling me we were responsible for everything that's gone wrong in Publicity over the past two years. He swore it must be one of us who sent the photos of the Eight Fifty to France."

" Why that?" asked Bill, in a voice that expressed his worry.

" Why?" Parry whacked the ruler up and down on the palm of his left hand. " Because he wanted to blame us for everything."

" Didn't you tell him he was being a b.f.?"

The ruler became motionless. " One doesn't speak to a superior like that."

" I suppose he asked you who was favourite in the murder stakes?"

The ruler moved very quickly. " I never listen to gossip."

" Surely the police were on to you over the week-end?"

" A detective inspector did visit me."

" Then I'll guarantee one thing, Oswald. He showed interest in only two people. George and myself. Didn't you mention that to the maharaja?"

" Naturally not."

There was a knock on the door and Corinne Hammer came in. When she saw Bill, her expression became sullen and angry.

" Yes, Miss Hammer?" said Parry.

" Mr. Togliati will be telephoning you soon from Milan, Mr. Parry. You asked me to remind you."

" Thanks."

She remained standing by the doorway.

" That's all," said Parry, with unusual sharpness. He watched her leave. When the door was shut, he said : " I sometimes wish she was just a little less . . . less overwhelmingly determined to be perfect. My wife calls her my saintly alter ego."

" What did Andover finally say?"

Parry shrugged his shoulders. " He was full of complaints, but nothing else. From one little thing he let drop, I gathered his wife had given him an uncomfortable week-end. Have you ever met her?"

" No."

" She's the kind of woman who runs the local Mothers' Union."

:: ::

Detective Inspector Shute travelled to London by car. At the police station, he was met by a detective chief inspector.

" You were lucky," said the detective chief inspector, as soon as they were both in his office. " The envelope was faulty and the machine operator discovered the fault after only a thousand envelopes. She had the machine repaired but, being on piece-work, she let the faulty thousand go through. The firm traced the consignment to their wholesaler for south-west and west London. He sold it to a shop."

" And then, sir?"

" I sent a chap along to have a word with the owner of the shop. The thousand envelopes had been a special order and had been delivered to the customer the day after they arrived. This customer buys two thousand envelopes every month."

Shute leaned forward in his chair, which creaked loudly. " Does the shopkeeper know the name?"

" Heavers. His family have lived in the district for a number of years. He's respectable and respected, in so far as anyone is in this day and age."

Shute pulled a packet of cigarettes from out of his pocket. He offered it to the other, who refused. " Mind if I do?" He lit a cigarette. " It has all the markings of a false trail, then?"

" Heavers has a beautiful old house which kind of Georgian to me, a nice-looking wife, and a son at Charterhouse. A thousand to one he votes Conservative. If we rub him up the wrong way, we'll be buried well out of sight of our pensions."

" Why should he want two thousand envelopes a month?"

" I could suggest a score of reasons. Hon. Sec. of something or other."

" What's his job?"

The detective chief inspector opened a drawer and took from it a sheet of paper which he read. " He was in insurance. Three years ago, he quit."

" And since then?"

" Not known."

" Has he been left money?"

" Perhaps. Those kind of people collect rich relations."

Shute searched for an ash-tray and the other pushed one across. " I'd like to talk to him."

" You realise it'll have to be entirely your pigeon?"

" I'll take full responsibility, sir."

" I'll send my D.I. along with you as liaison."

Shute smiled sarcastically. " Or to report back on what kind of a B.U. I make?"

A quarter of an hour later, Shute and Detective Inspector Vernon drove the half mile which brought them to a road in which large houses were set in large and well-kept gardens.

" Nice spot," said Shute.

" All right for them that can afford it," replied Vernon. They parked in front of shut garage doors numbered 46. They went in to the garden. Shute noticed the perfect order of everything. The lawn had been cut within the past twenty-four hours and he could not see a weed in the beds on either side of the stone path or the three rose beds. In front of the house were parked an Austin Healey Sprite and a 3.8 Jaguar. " Both theirs?" he asked.

Vernon shook his head. " I don't know."

When they reached the front door, Shute knocked. There was a short wait before it was opened by a young woman in an attractive plain frock. She smiled. " Yes, please?"

Norwegian, thought Shute. "Is Mr. Heavers in, please?" Two cars, a Norwegian girl to help in the house, and probably a gardener—Heavers had plenty of money to spend. "We're two police officers and we'd like to speak to Mr. Heavers for a moment or two."

She asked them to wait and very carefully shut the door on them.

"Afraid we're going to pinch the family silver," said Vernon sourly.

Their wait was very short. The door was opened and a man in his early forties, dressed in a country suit of a light heather colour, faced them. His body was tending towards fat without, as yet, definitely being fat. "You want to speak to me?"

"Yes please, sir," said Shute.

"I'm rather busy."

"We won't keep you long."

Heavers stepped aside and the two detectives entered the house. At the end of the passage beyond the hall, carpeted with an Indian rug, a woman stepped out of a room and looked at them. Heavers smiled at her as he led them into a sitting-room in which Scandinavian furniture had been carefully chosen to blend with the three pieces of very good Regency furniture.

"Sit down," said Heavers, as he indicated the easy-chairs.

"I'm from Kent, sir," said Shute. "Leamarsh."

Heavers sat in a rocking chair. "The only time I've been in Kent in the past five years is when I've motored down to Lydd to catch the air ferry."

"We've unfortunately just had a murder."

"Of course! Leamarsh sounded familiar. Wasn't that the girl who was killed in the car factory after some dance, or other?"

"That's right."

"I doubt I'll be of much help. I bought a Lanfair

in nineteen-fifty. Memory tells me it did manage to hold more or less together until nineteen-fifty-two when it finally expired just outside the Savoy. Since then, I've concentrated on other breeds."

"A Jaguar and an Austin Healey?"

"That's right, Inspector . . . I'm sorry, I didn't quite catch your name?"

"Shute."

"Of course. Frankly, I don't understand the reason for this visit and as I'm rather busy . . ." As he allowed his voice to die away, he looked quickly at Vernon, who was studying with openly expressed criticism an original Bacon on the wall.

"I've been told you're no longer in insurance, sir?" Shute spoke slowly, carefully trying to walk the tight-rope between an ineffectual interrogation and one which, should Heavers be innocent, would land him in trouble.

"Well?"

"Do you work at home now?"

"What the devil is this? What gives you the right to come in here asking me these questions?"

"I thought I'd explained, sir. I'm investigating a murder."

"Which, obviously, can't have anything to do with me."

"That's not exactly certain, sir."

"Why not?"

"Do you buy two thousand envelopes a month?" Heavers slowly began to rock the chair.

"I thought you might like to tell me about them?"

They were silent. From the hall, came the chimes of the grandmother clock striking six o'clock. There was a rustling sound which it took Shute several seconds to identify as the noise caused by the rocker moving against the thick-pile carpet.

Shute still did not know whether this was the man who had handled the envelope in which had been the

F

fifty pounds. If it finally proved to be he, then a beautiful home and a happy family were going to be destroyed.

They heard the sounds of female voices. The rocker kept on rocking.

Shute suffered an itching in the back of his neck. He longed to scratch it, but he forced himself to remain motionless.

Slowly, the rocker came to a halt.

Shute watched Heavers's face. He could see that any spirit of defiance had gone and that only sick fear remained. This, then, was the man they were after. This, then, was going to be a tragedy. "We know most of the story," he murmured.

Heavers licked his lips. He stared straight ahead of himself. "What does it mean?"

"So far as you're concerned?"

"Yes."

"I can't say. Quite a lot could depend on what sort of co-operation we receive."

"It can't have anything to do with the murder."

"The dead girl had an envelope in her handbag. It contained fifty one-pound notes."

"Well?" Heavers lit a cigarette.

"The murderer had been taking photographs. Pretty nasty ones." Shute put his hand in his pocket and brought out an envelope from which he took several prints. He passed them to Heavers. At first, Heavers refused to look down at them, but eventually he did so. He handed them back.

"What did she get paid for this?" asked Shute.

"God, how should I know?"

"You do."

"Why did you come to me?"

"We traced the envelope back to you."

The door opened and Mrs. Heavers entered. She was dressed in a summer frock which was not so simple that it hid the fact it was an expensive one: she had a large solitaire diamond ring on her engagement finger: her face and hair had the pleasant, smooth appearance that came from constant expert attention. " I wondered if you'd like some coffee . . ." She suddenly stopped speaking as she stared at her husband's face. " What's wrong?" she asked.

" Don't worry," said Heavers.

" But what's happened?"

" I'll tell you later on. Go out for now, will you, Betty."

Shute knew that she had recognised, instinctively, that something had come to ruin for all times the pleasant life that had been hers.

" Can I have a drink?" asked Heavers.

" Of course," replied Shute. He wished he had not seen the wife's face as she left the room.

Heavers went across to the cocktail cabinet and poured himself out a whisky.

" How did you come to know her?" asked Shute.

" Who?" Heavers drank too quickly and some of the whisky ran down the sides of his mouth.

" Sheila Jones."

" I didn't know her."

" She had one of your envelopes. The photographs of her were for you."

Heavers finished the drink and poured himself another.

" Don't you think it would be much easier to get it all over and done with now?" suggested Shute quietly.

Heavers returned to the rocker and sat down. He began to rock. " I was twenty years in insurance." He drank. " I'd worked hard and long and I was lined up for a directorship, which really meant something. Then the firm was taken-over. We were assured nothing would change and our seniority would remain exactly as it was, but after twelve months I'd seen two men from the other company promoted over my head and when I complained I was told I had as good as had it. The top jobs were for the men from the senior firm.

" One day, the first man to be promoted over my head showed me a ' sporting print.' It didn't amuse me : that sort of thing never has. But when he told me it cost him ten shillings and he was on a regular mailing list, I began to think about the money someone was making."

Heavers finished his drink. " I started up business. In six months, I had a mailing list of three hundred, in a year it was a thousand. Soon, it was two thousand. Two thousand men eager to pay five or ten shillings for a ' sporting print' every month. The photograph cost me a hundred and fifty or three hundred. There was the cost of reproducing the prints and mailing, but the rest was clear profit. It's been worth six thousand a year."

As Heavers remained silent, Shute spoke. " And Sheila Jones?"

" Was she . . . Are you sure she was the girl in the photographs?"

" Quite certain."

" If only I'd listened to my bloody instincts . . ." He cleared his throat. " I got a letter asking me if I wanted any photographs and if so I was to insert an answer in the personal column of *The Times*. There was always difficulty getting the raw material for the trade." He spoke with an open contempt that was directed solely at himself. " Instinct told me not to touch the letter in case it was some sort of a trap, or a lunatic, but I put the advert in. I had another letter telling me to say how much I'd pay."

" Who were the letters from?"

" They were typed and unsigned."

" I take it you haven't kept them?"

" I kept them. The whole thing became much odder when I came to pay the first hundred and fifty. I was told to put the money in an envelope and leave it in a hollow tree at the east end of Hyde Park. It was like playing spies."

" So you put the money there?"

" Yes."

" But didn't wait to see who collected it?"

" I tried, because the whole thing was so fantastic. I waited for an hour and no one went near the tree so I gave up. The next time I waited for an hour and a half with the same result. Then I gave up worrying."

" How many photographs of this girl have you had?"

" Something under a dozen."

" Were they always like the ones I've shown you?"

" Roughly."

" Was there never a man as well?"

" No."

" Then they only retailed at five shillings?"

Heavers lifted his glass to his lips, but he had already emptied it. He was looking old.

" I want those two letters," said Shute. " And I want to see the other photographs of her. Are they in the house?"

" Here? D'you think I'd risk Betty . . ." He stopped abruptly.

Ten minutes later, they left the house and drove in the police car to a road in which were a number of small shops. Heavers's " office " was above a tobacconist. When asked to open the small loose-standing safe, he silently took a key from his pocket, knelt down, and opened it. He brought out an album in grey covers on the front of which was printed, " Your Holiday Snaps." He handed this to Shute.

The photographs of Sheila Jones were easily identified. In each case her head was turned away, but the youth of her body was in striking contrast to the age-filled bodies of the other women.

" Let's have the letters," said Shute.

Still without speaking, Heavers searched inside the

safe. Eventually, he found them and gave them to Shute.

There was no address, date, or signature, on either of the typewritten letters.

"Did you bother to examine the postmark?" asked Shute.

"It was Maidstone both times."

"I'll take these with me, Mr. Heavers. And that album."

"And I'll bother you for a list of your customers," said Vernon, in a contemptuous voice.

Heavers blinked rapidly.

CHAPTER IX

XXXXXXXXXXXXXXXXXXXXXXXXXXXXXXXXXXXXXXXXXXXXXXXXXXX

BILL ARRIVED home at six-twenty in the evening. As he garaged his car and walked towards the house, his father appeared. It was not until later that it occurred to him that his father had been waiting.

"How's the day been, Bill?"

He came to a halt. "How's any day at Lanfairs? Chaos and confusion."

"I meant . . . Anything more about the murder?" Henry Stemple scraped his boot against the edge of an old apple tree and removed a large clod of dung.

"Apart from the fact that some of the staff regard me as a cross between Dracula and Frankenstein, there might not have been one for all the effect it's had."

"Frankenstein's monster," corrected Henry Stemple, automatically, and unaware he had done so. "Weren't the police about?"

"No."

" Maybe that means they've discovered someone entirely unconnected with Lanfairs?"

" Maybe."

" Your mother's very worried, Bill. We know you didn't . . . That is . . ." Henry Stemple gave up trying to say what he wanted to say without really saying it.

" I told you I had nothing to do with it. Good God, I don't go around the country hitting women over the head."

" It's terribly unfortunate that you were down in the photography room beforehand."

" And that's not an original thought!" Bill laughed shortly.

" Try and understand that your mother's only worrying on your behalf, Bill." Henry Stemple altered the conversation. " What's wrong with the staff?"

Bill took a packet of cigarettes from his pocket. They both smoked. " Some of them seem to recoil from my presence. A dishonoured murderer, if you will," he misquoted. His voice became angry. " Some people would hang on a suspicion. I was down in the photography room with Sheila. When we left, she was alive. I went straight upstairs, drank too much, and came home after a brush with the law. That's all I know, but does that suit the sanctimonious bastards?"

" Has it been very bad?"

Bill shrugged his shoulders. " Most of it's in the mind, as the Goons would have said. But Corinne Hammer tries not to breathe the same air and Pat White stares at me with an avid interest."

" It'll all come to an end as soon as they discover who it was."

" Of course." Bill dropped his cigarette on to the ground and stamped it out. " I've been smoking too much. I'll end up in a bottle in a pathological museum."

He looked at his father. " Have you thought about the murder?"

" Little else."

" Does it really seem possible it was someone from outside? Can you imagine someone happening to enter the building and happening to go down to the photography room where Sheila happens to be?"

His father did not answer.

" No one really believes it was an outsider." Bill began to walk towards the house. His father kept in step with him. " Why did she have to involve me in it?" he demanded, with irrational anger.

" Let's go and have a bottle of champagne."

Bill stopped. He looked at his father. " You must reckon the situation's pretty bloody bad."

Later that night, and once he was in bed, Bill lay on his back and stared up at the beamed ceiling. There were seven cross beams on either side of the much larger central beam. When he had been ill two years before with an unidentified fever, he had counted and recounted those beams because in some strange way they were reality. Now, they again became reality. They had been there for 400 years and with no more than ordinary luck they would be there for the next 400. The fears which he had been suffering over the death of Sheila were transitory and therefore unreality. He knew he was innocent, which meant everything. The law of England defended the innocent and punished the guilty. If he was innocent, then nothing and nobody could ever prove he was guilty.

:: ::

Carthwright walked, with his usual arrogance, into Bill's office on Tuesday morning. " I've done that article."

Bill looked up from the revised itinerary for the forthcoming visit of Italian journalists. " What article?"

" Jesus, man, you'll next be asking who Lloyd Llanfaider was." Carthwright dropped four sheets of paper, clipped together, on to the desk. " The old, tired, and sad story of the five thousand. You told me to beat it again. So I beat. It reads like it had the bloom of age."

" No one can accuse you of trying to sell your work."

" D'you reckon I'll break my brains for this outfit? I'm telling you, if they had a genius in the place they'd shout for a fumigation. Look at 'em in nineteen-fifty. Front-wheel drive? Never. The sun will set on the British Empire before Lanfairs desecrate their noble name by employing so foreign a device. Come the sixties and they prepare to announce their revolutionary front-wheel drive Eight Fifty."

" Maybe they reckon the sun's set. O.K., Jim, I'll read it through when I've time."

Carthwright sat down. " Not exactly a ray of sunshine, are you?"

" No?"

" Did you know old Gurren is offering two to one it's you?"

Bill spoke with bitter anger. " I'll sue him . . ."

" Show some sense and put some money down. That is, of course, if it wasn't you."

Bill's anger turned into fear, caused by the knowledge that Gurren, never one to spend an unnecessary penny, was so openly certain of his guilt.

Carthwright continued speaking. " Janet reckons it was the maharaja. She says the old bastard has that kind of a look about him. Don't see he looks very much different to any other gormless Englishman." Carthwright stood up. " Back to the work bench."

The telephone rang and Bill picked up the receiver. Mrs. Berry told him two policemen wanted to see him. Should she send them up? He told her, yes.

" Flatties?" asked Carthwright.

" What?"

"Flatties. The reasonably disrespectful name for detectives." Carthwright crossed to the door. "Give them my love." He left.

Bill picked up the itinerary and put it down again. He had known the police would interview him, he knew he had no need to fear such interview, yet now there was a churning sensation in his stomach.

At all costs, he must appear calm. They would be looking for signs of worry, so he must show none.

There was a knock on his door and Mrs. Berry opened it. As she stepped back to let two men enter, she stared at him with unflattering attention.

He had seen neither of the detectives before. One of them was a barrel of a man about whose movements, strangely, there was no sense of awkwardness.

"'Morning, Mr. Stemple. I'm Detective Inspector Shute. This is Detective Constable Tripp."

The detective constable, a lugubrious man in his middle fifties, nodded his head.

"We're hoping you'll be able to help us a little, Mr. Stemple."

Bill shrugged his shoulders and was then certain the gesture must have appeared ridiculous. He sat down. The D.I. had the kind of pale watchful eyes which always seemed to be trying to see round the corners of a person's mind.

"Cigarette?" asked Shute.

Bill leaned across and went to take a cigarette. Something happened so that the cigarette case fell on to the desk. He picked it up.

"Help yourself, Mr. Stemple."

He did so and then returned the case. He was momentarily intrigued by the way the detective accepted it, arching his hand and holding only the edges, but his mind really only had room for the forthcoming interview. A gas lighter was flicked open for him.

" You kindly made a statement to one of my officers."
Shute sat down. " I wondered if you'd anything to
add?"

" Should I have?"

Shute smiled. " We usually find witnesses forget something in their first statement. Some little thing which
they remember later on."

" I mentioned everything."

" Oh, well, it shows you've a good memory! You're
quite positive, then, that the last time you saw Miss
Jones was when you were at the top of the basement
stairs when she went back for her handbag?"

" Yes." Bill had meant to say no more, but some
inner compulsion forced him to continue. " I left her
and went to the bar."

" And you didn't see her again?"

" No."

The D.I. looked straight at Bill. " I wonder if you'd
clear up one final point for me? Where did you get
the two hundred pounds in one-pound notes you paid
into your bank in Ashford last week?"

The question shocked Bill so much that for several
seconds his mind was a jumble of incoherent thoughts.
As he struggled to clear his mind, he met the gaze
of those eyes. He hurriedly looked away. Amidst all
the confusion, there was one truth which he must never
forget: the source of that money must never be revealed because if it were he would be ignominiously
sacked from Lanfairs. " That money's nothing to do
with you. I mean, it's nothing to do with her . . . her
death."

" You'll have to accept my word that there may be a
connection."

" There can't be."

" Perhaps I should explain, Mr. Stemple, that the
murderer was taking pornographic photographs of Sheila
Jones. He received a hundred and fifty pounds for each

one accepted and out of this he paid fifty pounds to the dead girl."

Bill felt he had moved into a world where logic held no place. " She . . . she wouldn't do anything like that. She was far too nice."

" We have the photographs."

Bill struggled first to accept what he had been told, then to find an answer to the question of the two hundred pounds. In the end, he could only say: " I won that money."

" Where?"

Bill's mind threatened to panic. Where the hell had there been racing the previous week? Then, he remembered that friends of his parents had been to the Folkestone races. " Folkestone."

" I suppose you couldn't tell us which bookmaker you won this considerable sum from?" asked Shute and his voice did not sound sarcastic.

Bill shook his head. If he stuck to a story as simple as the one he had just given, surely they could never prove him a liar?

Shute leaned forward and flicked the ash from his cigarette into the ash-tray.

" That girl couldn't have been Sheila," said Bill suddenly. " She wasn't like that at all."

" Comparison measurements have proved it was her. In any case, there were several shots of her posing in the camera found in the dark-room." Shute scratched his nose. " We had a check on her savings. She banked four hundred pounds in the past twelve months and had another fifty in her handbag. That could not have come from her salary. Money tempts a lot of people."

Sheila had always liked money. Bill remembered the pleasure she had gained from eating at expensive restaurants: a pleasure quite distinct from that given by the food. But Sheila posing for dirty photos?

" What notepaper do you use here?" asked Shute.

"Notepaper?" Once again, Bill was struggling to alert his mind to a new subject.

"What paper do you use for typing? Could you show me a piece?"

Bill pulled open one of the drawers on his right and brought out several sheets of quarto paper. He handed them across.

Shute picked up one piece and held it up to catch the light from the window. Then, he lowered it and twisted round on the chair to look at the second desk and the typewriter on it. "Do you use that typewriter?"

"Yes."

"Does anyone else?"

"My secretary. That is, whichever girl comes up from the typing pool."

"May I use it?"

"Why? I don't understand . . ."

"Shan't be a minute." Shute stood up and crossed to the second desk. He removed the cover from the typewriter. "I've never graduated beyond two fingers and a thumb." He wound the paper round. "And the thumb can't manage anything but the space bar. What about you, Tripp?"

Tripp spoke for the first time. "I can't go anywhere with the thumb, sir." His dull voice was thick with Cockney twang.

"Why are you typing?" asked Bill.

"A routine check, Mr. Stemple."

"Checking what?"

"Whether this machine typed a letter to a Mr. Heavers." Shute began to type unrhythmically, but with considerable speed.

"Who's Heavers?" asked Bill desperately. The clacking of the typewriter went on. "Who's Heavers?" he shouted.

Shute stopped typing. "The man who was sending out the photographs," he said, as if the need for the question surprised him. He stared at what he had typed, unwound the paper, folded it into four, and put it in his inside pocket. He stood up. "Have you had any second thoughts about the two hundred pounds?"

"I won it at the races."

"Right. Thanks for your co-operation, Mr. Stemple. Very helpful."

Bill watched the detectives leave the room. The door closed.

He cursed himself, his stupidity, and the photograph of the Lanfair 850. When he had taken it, his act had seemed to be a lark : later, when the money arrived, it had appeared stupid : now, it had become frightening. No matter what happened he dare not disclose its source.

How could Sheila have allowed herself to be used for those kind of photographs? He remembered the skilful way in which she had fought off any and all of his advances.

Was it George? Had she and George been making money? He remembered that when she and he, Bill, had left the photography room, she had said she thought she saw George. If things became too black, he would have to tell the police that George had probably been down in the basement.

He leaned back in the chair and felt sick. Because he had fooled around with her, he had become a suspect.

It was a shock to realise she had died only four days ago.

::   ::

Detective Superintendent Easdale took a plastic phial from his pocket and emptied out of it two small pink pills. He swallowed the pills with the aid of some coffee.

"So at the moment," said Shute, "it's a case of waiting for those two reports."

"Why aren't they through?"

" I wouldn't know, sir. I asked for them to be priority."

Easdale sat down behind Shute's desk. He always made himself at home in other people's rooms. " The case ought to be open and shut by now."

" I don't think we're doing too badly. It's a long way to go before a week's up." Shute crossed to the mantelpiece and leaned against it. He stared at the patch of peeling plaster on the opposite wall.

Easdale finished his coffee. " Most of the Press spelled my name wrong."

" So I saw." So far as the Press was concerned, thought Shute, the great Easdale was the only policeman of any consequence in the case.

There was a knock on the door and a police cadet, with the kind of angelic-looking face that spelled trouble, entered. " This has just come through for you, sir." He handed Shute a large brown envelope.

Easdale studied the cadet. " Your top button's undone."

" Yes, sir."

" Then do the bloody thing up."

" Very good, sir." The cadet did up the button with an exaggerated care that was only just not insolent. Then he left the room.

Shute slit open the envelope and took out a typed report. He read through it very quickly, then looked up. " It's from H.Q., sir. The finger-print on the camera tripod was Stemple's. The letters sent to Heavers were typed on paper identical to that Stemple gave me and the typewriter now in his office was the one used."

" That's that, then."

" I suppose it is, sir. When I put this evidence before the legal boys, I doubt they'll hesitate about prosecuting."

" Then why the devil d'you sound so worried?"

Shute moved away from the mantelpiece and crossed

to his desk. He opened a Maori carved wooden cigarette box.

"Everything fits, doesn't it?" snapped Easdale.

"So far as I can see. Except for one thing."

"What's that?"

"The girl was considered to be a bit of a prude. We know she was a virgin, so Stemple never got that far with her. Yet she allowed him to take those photographs. It doesn't fit."

"Don't be so bloody daft. What a woman makes out she is and what she actually is are two totally different things. The most ladylike woman I've ever met worked a beat in Margate during the season. At fifty quid a go, I reckon even you'd start posing." Easdale suddenly laughed. It was a strange sound.

: :   : :

The police arrested Bill only minutes after he arrived home. Margaret Stemple, weeding the bed of mesembry-anthemums, saw the police car turn into the drive. She stopped speaking to him and stared at the approaching car with a look of hate and fear.

Detective Inspector Shute was very polite. He gave the usual warning, after which he asked Bill if he would like to collect his toilet things and a pair of pyjamas. Detective Constable Marrins went with Bill into the house.

"He didn't have anything to do with it," declared Margaret Stemple, in a voice that was shrill.

"I'm very sorry, madam," said Shute, with more than mere formal politeness.

Seven minutes later, as they watched the police car drive away, Henry Stemple put his arm round his wife's shoulder. He felt her body begin to jerk as she cried.

"He didn't do it," she said fiercely. "He swore to me he didn't."

He spoke very sadly. "I hope to God that's the truth."

She pulled away from his side. " You're calling him a liar."

He remembered how much evidence he already knew there was against his son and he imagined how much more there must be in the police's hands. He did not dare to judge his son.

   : :   : :

Michael P. Andover, director of Publicity, hammered his desk with the flat of his hand. " What's it going to do to us?" He was a short, fat man whose face had lined so deeply that he looked an over-aged voluptuary.

Oswald Parry nervously shook his head.

" It's in every single paper. First the wretched girl gets herself killed in this building, then Stemple is arrested. What the hell does it make Lanfair Motors look like? I'll tell you. Like a bunch of murdering sadists. The British can stand anything but this and they'll stop buying Lanfair cars."

" I don't think . . ." began Parry.

" Don't argue. Maybe you didn't read the paper which called the dance an orgy? What would Lloyd Llanfaider have said about that?"

Parry did not try to answer that interesting question.

" Get this straight. Our first job is to wipe out the image of sex that's formed in the public's mind. Tell the Press that Stemple was engaged on false references . . ."

" We have to be careful of libel, Mr. Andover."

" Don't you start telling me what we've got to be careful of. By God, I'm telling you that if the image isn't changed right smartly there'll be changes in the staff. I want the name of Lanfair to become as pure as it always was. I don't care how you do it, but do it. Is that clear?"

" Yes, sir."

" The board of directors will be watching very closely, Parry."

Parry left and took the lift from the second to the third floor. As he entered his own office, he was greeted by Corinne Hammer.

"Is everything all right, Mr. Parry?" she asked anxiously.

"Not too bad." He often wondered what he had done to inspire such devotion in her. He had once put the question to his wife who had laughed so much she had choked.

"How was Mr. Andover, Mr. Parry?"

"In several of his more difficult moods." He sat down. "Would you care to ask Mr. Carthwright to come in here?"

"He shouldn't have done it," she said shrilly. "Mr. Stemple shouldn't have done it."

"Would you ask Mr. Carthwright?"

"Of course, Mr. Parry. But it's all wrong that you should have to go to Mr. Andover." She left.

Parry rubbed his eyes. Presuming the public image of Lanfair Motors had been injured, which he did not, what in the name of hell could anyone do to try to salvage it?

Carthwright came into the room. "The old girl said you wanted me?"

Parry spoke quickly, trying to cover the nervousness which affected all his dealings with Carthwright. "Will you take over Mr. Stemple's duties for the moment, please. I'd like you to take special note of the next journalists' visit."

"Sure."

"Have you any idea who's coming?"

"The Wops."

"Of course. Rather flamboyant people. They usually smell."

"Foreigners usually think the English smell."

Parry blinked rapidly. "Do they?" he finally said.

" Not giving him much of a chance, are you?" snapped Carthwright.

Parry sighed. " I hope you won't make things any more difficult than they already are."

" Jesus! Isn't there anyone in the whole crumbling building willing to stand up for him?"

Parry was determined not to be drawn further. " Mr. Andover says we must try to eradicate the bad image of sexual depravity Lanfair Motors have gained through this unfortunate case. He doesn't want the cars to become an unfortunate sex symbol. He suggests a subtle approach to the Press might help."

" And I suggest he needs his flamin' brains tested," said Carthwright, with typical directness.

: :   : :

Bill paced the cell in which they had locked him.

The hearing before the magistrates was over and he was committed to the next Assize in the middle of October on a charge of murdering Sheila Jones.

From the small dock, he had heard witness after witness giving evidence against him. Because depositions had had to be made out, evidence had been so slowly given that he had found his mind had wandered at times to the extent that he had missed some of the proceedings. Yet it was this evidence, much of it from people he knew well, that might convict him.

After the first day's hearing, he had slept badly during the night. Within him had been the terrible and painful cry of innocence.

After the second, and final, day's hearing the cry had become one of utter despair. Who was going to believe him against such an enormous weight of evidence?

He paced the cell. He had not killed her. Innocence could not be convicted in a court of law.

CHAPTER X

XXXXXXXXXXXXXXXXXXXXXXXXXXXXXXXXXXXXXXXXXXXXXXXXXXXX

HENRY STEMPLE drove into Ashford and parked in the council car-park. He walked up the narrow passage past the Odeon and into the High Street. He looked at his watch. A quarter of an hour to go before his appointment—it took tragedy to make him early.

He crossed the road. As he came level with the Saracen's Head, he noticed two women who seemed to be staring at him. They spoke to each other. Clacking old hens, he thought bitterly. "That's *his* father! He smashed her skull in because she wouldn't . . ."

He went into Geerings and collected a book that had been ordered for him. He imagined everyone was talking about him. When he left, it was time to go straight to the solicitor's.

The waiting-room was decorated in contemporary colours and because he loved the softness of age, he was repelled by them. Fortunately, his wait was a short one. Within three minutes, he was shaking hands with Marshden.

"Have a seat, Henry." Marshden, dressed in black coat and striped trousers, indicated a comfortable leather chair.

"Well?" said Stemple, as he sat down.

"I'm going to give it to you without the sugar. The evidence as brought out in the magistrates' court was sufficient in the absence of a very strong defence, to convict Bill. Up to now I can't see any defence worth talking about."

Henry Stemple stared at the nearer of the two glass-fronted cabinets filled with text books. " You're saying that Bill did it and he'll be convicted."

" I'm saying he will be convicted."

" Pat, you know as well as I do that he swears he knows nothing about her death. If he'd killed her, he'd have told us. He'd never have lied to Margaret."

There was a silence.

" What are you going to do?" asked Henry Stemple dully.

" Brief the best counsel available. Beyond that . . ." Marshden tapped the desk with his fingers. " I'm a conservative type of a bloke," he said slowly.

Stemple looked at him without understanding.

" After thirty or more years of ministering to the legal needs of the mainly law-abiding inhabitants of this market town, I'm more than settled in outlook. Leila says I'm the most conventional man she's ever met."

" What does it matter . . ."

Marshden held up his right hand. " I've handled this case so far because I've been your lawyer for many, many years and because I'll do anything to help your family. But after thinking things over, I'm certain I'm not the right man simply and solely because I am so thunderingly conventional. If, and God knows it's a small if, there is any hope for Bill I'm certain it won't be a conventional one." He leaned forward. " Henry, I want you and Bill to agree to Joshua Tring taking over from me."

Stemple stared at him in astonishment. " But you've always said you've never been quite certain about him."

" When I accepted him as a partner, I did so knowing he wouldn't be an easy man to get on with. For the private records, I'd underrated the difficulty. I also correctly reckoned he wasn't an especially good lawyer."

" Then . . ."

" Joshua's father was a very great friend of mine.

Joshua was captured at Arnhem. He suffered hell in the prisoner-of-war camp because he insisted from the beginning that his captors must observe every single provision of the Geneva Conventions. It didn't matter that it was obviously quite illogical and even stupid to stand out for his and other people's rights to the extent that he did, he stood out. He was beaten up several times, his injured leg went bad. His life was saved only by the rapid advance of the Americans. The American doctor who saw him said his leg must be amputated: Joshua said no one was going to amputate any of his possessions. Somehow, he survived—with both legs. When he returned to England he was offered what he considered to be the wrong disability pension. He stormed the walls of bureaucracy for so long that part of them tumbled down from exhaustion and he was given the pension he knew was the right one. I believe the difference was one shilling and tenpence a week." Marshden folded his arms. " If Joshua is persuaded that Bill is innocent but that the whole world holds him guilty, Bill will have someone fighting for him who knows only one end to a fight. The end he considers to be just."

" But you said he wasn't a very good lawyer."

" He's too emotional. He tends to evaluate human rights with justice. In this case, there won't be enough law to matter."

" Suppose he fights all day and all night, every day and every night. Will it do any good?"

Marshden spoke slowly. " I doubt it, Henry. But there's always the faintest possibility that a completely unconventional approach could do some good."

" I'd sign a pact with the devil, if he'd help," said Henry Stemple.

: :   : :

Bill met Tring in the prison conference room. It was on the third floor of A block and through the barred window one had a clear view of the high brick wall that separated the prison from the town, servitude from freedom, abnormality from normalcy. Bill looked out and saw, beyond the wall, the top of a double-decker bus. He swallowed heavily.

He studied Tring. He saw a man with very black, wiry hair, a face which looked rather sad when in repose, a neat black moustache, a scarred chin, and a suit which would have been more appropriate to a point-to-point meeting than the present conference.

Tring came forward, limping slightly. " Good morning, Mr. Stemple."

The warder said : " All right, gentlemen?" He withdrew and the door clicked shut.

" I've come to take over from Patrick, if there are no objections from you?" Tring spoke in an abrupt tone of voice.

Bill unknowingly repeated the gist of his father's words of the day before. " I'd accept the devil's help if it would be any use."

" You don't think it would?"

" Would anything?"

" It depends whether you killed the girl, or not."

" Haven't I denied it enough times yet? How many does it have to be before just someone believes me?" Bill controlled his voice. " Since everyone knows I'm guilty, I can't think why they're bothering with the farce of a trial."

" What happened in the basement?"

Bill sat down in one of the four chairs grouped round the table. " I tried hard enough. But I wouldn't whisper the magic word ' marriage ' so she held on to all she possessed."

" Your intentions were strictly dishonourable, then?"

" Yes."

Tring sat down. He opened his brief-case and took from it a file. " Were you taking the photographs?"

" No."

" All right. Then where did the two hundred quid you paid into your bank come from?"

Bill took a packet of cigarettes from his pocket. " Have one?"

" I'll stick to a pipe." Tring picked up a pencil. " Where did the two hundred quid come from?"

" I won it at the Folkestone races."

" That's all balls."

Bill's face flushed.

" If you can't give me the truth," said Tring, " it's no damned good my trying to defend you. Were you taking the photos, but didn't kill her?"

" No."

" Where did the money come from?"

" What's it matter? It's got nothing to do with the case."

" Are you that much of a fool?" Tring closed the file and put it in his brief-case.

" I didn't kill her. I didn't kill her."

" So you claim."

Bill spoke with desperation. " In a few weeks' time, the new Lanfair Eight Fifty is coming out. One of the prototypes was in the research and experimental section and I went in to have a look at it. When I was inside, I suddenly realised I'd got my miniature Japanese camera in my pocket and no one else was in the place. I took three photographs of the car and they developed well. Like a b.f. I thought it would be fun to send copies to one of the French magazines. Call it a childish snook at authority. Back came two hundred pounds."

" Why didn't you tell the police this?"

" Isn't that obvious? Lanfairs are trying to find out who leaked the photo in order to sack him."

" But you think that as a convicted murderer they'll keep you on their payroll?"

" I didn't kill her. An innocent man can't be found guilty."

" Can't he?"

" They won't listen to me. I keep telling them the truth, but they're certain I'm lying."

Tring knew that feeling. The knowledge that one was in the right, but that no one else recognised the fact.

Bill spoke more calmly. " If I admit the truth about the photos, I've had it with Lanfairs whatever happens."

Tring tapped the pencil up and down on the thumb-nail of his left hand. " Just how much weight does the evidence of the two hundred pounds carry when stacked up against everything else?" He looked up. " That's the first major point to check with counsel."

::   ::

Allenbury, counsel for the prosecution, was a strongly built man whose stoop took several inches from his height. This, and the spectacles he sometimes wore, gave him much of the presence of a rather dusty school teacher. His presentation of a case was almost invariably dull because he treated all jurymen as un-intelligent and he therefore explained everything in great detail and at great length. Yet, if his speeches were dull, they were also deadly because he missed not a single point in the prosecution's case.

" . . . Members of the jury," he said, " I want you to keep a very careful note of all the times in this case. The prosecution will show that the last moment at which anyone but the prisoner saw Sheila Jones alive was at about eleven o'clock on Friday night when Miss King and Mr. Carthwright met the prisoner and the de-ceased at the door by the head of the stairs leading down to the basement. From then onwards, Miss Jones van-ished. One hour later, a time no more strictly accurate than any of the others because for obvious reason no one was keeping a strict note of the time, the prisoner joined four people who were drinking. The prisoner was now on his own and he made no reference to Miss Jones. These four witnesses will say that he seemed extremely upset about something and that he drank very heavily. Miss King and Mr. Carthwright left and shortly afterwards the prisoner went out with Mr. Albert Breslow to the latter's car, in the car-park, where they drank beer. The prisoner left there in his own car at about twelve-thirty and he drove into Ashford at twelve-fifty. He was stopped by a policeman who decided he was drunk in charge of the car. I have to advise you that it was decided he was not drunk and no charge was made. He left the police station at one-thirty-three on Saturday morning.

" You will remember, members of the jury, that I told you medical evidence holds death to have been between eleven-thirty and one-thirty on Saturday morning. You will be told that these times are not scientific times : they are times that medical evidence suggests limit the period within which the deceased was murdered. Nevertheless, I must tell you that, although it is considered improbable she could have died before eleven-thirty or after one-thirty, it is possible. The prosecution, however, says that she died between eleven o'clock and midnight, or, accepting the medical evidence; between eleven-thirty and twelve o'clock . . ."

Mr. Justice Waring wondered why Allenbury thought it necessary to say the same thing over and over and over again? The judge's dark, thin face expressed a little of his annoyance, but he remained silent. He looked at the prisoner in the dock, sitting to the right of the warder, and felt sorry that such a person should find himself in such a position.

: :   : :

By three o'clock in the afternoon, the courtroom was very hot and stuffy. Counsel for both sides had hoped for an order from the Bench allowing them to remove their wigs, but none had come from a man who appeared to be oblivious of the discomfort of the heat.

Janet King was in the witness-box.

" You were in the photography room for how long?" asked Allenbury.

" I don't know." She looked at counsel with an expression of helplessness. " The time went so terribly quickly."

" I'm sure it did," said Allenbury sarcastically, as he looked down at his brief. " You and Mr. Carthwright then left?"

" We went up the stairs to go back to the dance and we met them at the top."

" Whom do you mean?"

" Bill and Sheila, of course."

" Was anything said by you to the accused?"

" I think I may have said the couch was comfortable." She suddenly appeared to be very worried. " But I don't want you to think . . ."

" I shouldn't concern yourself with Mr. Allenbury's thoughts," said the judge.

Allenbury half bowed. " On the principle, no doubt, my Lord, of *de minimis non curat lesc*?"

" I should prefer to say, Mr. Allenbury, *de non apparentibus, et non existentibus, eadem est ratio.*"

Allenbury addressed the witness again. " Miss King, did you see Miss Jones actually enter the photography room?"

" No, I didn't."

" Mr. Carthwright has testified that you were present when the prisoner arrived in the annex at about midnight. That is correct, is it?"

" I don't know what the time was. It goes so quickly."

" We have already heard how you found that so. Was anyone with the accused?"

" No."

" Did the prisoner mention Miss Jones at all?"

" I don't think so."

" How would you describe him at this time?"

" Well, he was just the same as usual, except I did notice his hair wasn't very tidy."

" You appear to have misunderstood my question, Miss King."

" Oh, dear, I'm terribly sorry. I really didn't mean to."

" How would you describe his general state?"

" His what?"

" Was he nervous?" said Allenbury, in exasperated tones of voice.

Gonchera, defending silk, stood up. " My learned friend really must not lead the witness so openly," he said, with ironic pleasantness.

" Who is leading whom?" murmured the judge.

Gonchera sat down. Allenbury fiddled with one of the leads of his gown. " Now, Miss King, and I endeavour for your sake to put the matter in its simplest terms, would you describe the prisoner's attitude towards you, towards the other people present, and the world in general?"

" He was very nice."

Allenbury sighed. " Very well," he said, with elaborate weariness. " What were you all doing?"

" Do you mean then or earlier?"

" Then. What were the four of you doing when the prisoner joined you?"

" We were having a drink."

" How many drinks did the prisoner have?"

" I don't really know."

" Other witnesses will say the number was either three or four, this within the space of fifteen minutes. Would you agree with this estimate?"

" Did he really have that many?" she asked, with a child-like innocence.

Allenbury took his spectacles from his pocket, put them

on, and then stared at Janet with what appeared to be growing disbelief. He took off his spectacles. " Perhaps you can remember just enough to say whether you or the prisoner left the group first?"

" Well, I did. That is, James and me."

" I doubt anyone seriously thought you departed on your own. After you had left, did you see the prisoner again?"

" No."

" Did you ever see Sheila Jones again?"

" No."

Allenbury had a word with his solicitor, after which he sat down.

Gonchera stood up. Despite a surname which marked his Turkish parentage, he had been born and educated in England. He was a man who persuaded juries and his soft voice and pleasant manner had often persuaded them to support his case when had they been more logical in their reasoning they would never have done so.

Tring, sitting in front of Gonchera, turned round. " The car-park," he said.

" Quite so." As a barrister, Gonchera would never have been rude to a solicitor who might brief him again in the future, but he had frequently suffered a strong desire to be more open in his dealings with Tring. He addressed the witness. " Miss King, you have stated you did not see the accused again. Did you speak to him, though, or did he speak to you?"

" I don't really know."

" Does that mean you did not speak to him, or that you spoke to someone and you can't be absolutely sure who it was?"

" Why not go on and give all the evidence yourself," said Allenbury loudly.

Gonchera smiled pleasantly.

Janet answered the question. " We were in the car-park by James's car, when someone said good night to us. I'm certain it was Bill."

" He must have been in a very reasonable state, then, to have recognised . . ."

Allenbury stood up. " When I suggested to my learned friend that he should give the evidence, my Lord, I suppose I should have made it clear that I was not, in fact, advocating such a course."

Gonchera sat down. He had made as much use of the evidence as he could.

Allenbury re-examined very briefly. " What were you and Mr. Carthwright doing outside his car?"

" Kissing," said Janet, in a whisper.

" What was that? Speak up, please."

" He was kissing me."

" Thoroughly?"

Janet managed to blush.

" Probably, your ability to recognise voices at such a moment was not at its sharpest, Miss King?" Allenbury sat down.

Vigen was called. He tried to give his evidence in a completely neutral manner. Gurren, who followed him, did not.

" We were drinking whisky. Bill Stemple joined us and he was in a terrible state."

" What exactly do you mean by that?" asked Allenbury. Gurren, enjoying his moment of notoriety, spoke quickly. " He was terribly nervous and sweating. He drank at least four whiskies so quickly it was obvious he was trying to forget something terrible."

" Just stick to the facts, please, and leave the jury to draw any conclusions."

Gurren looked hurt.

" Did he speak?"

" Not very much. He was too busy drinking."

" Presumably, all of you were drinking?"

" Not like he was."

" Did you see him again after he left you?"

" No, I didn't."

" When was the last time you saw the deceased?"

" It must have been around eleven o'clock."

Just before he cross-examined some ten minutes later, Gonchera turned and spoke to his junior, Geraldine Pawley, a woman of fifty-three who had for thirty years managed to gain considerable success in what was still almost essentially a masculine profession. Whilst he was talking to her, his gown was tugged. When he ignored the gesture, it was tugged again. He turned back. " Ye?" he said to Tring.

" This character was so sloshed he couldn't have told you how many arms he had," said Tring. " The man's a bloody liar."

" All witnesses are liars, Mr. Tring. It's merely a question of degree." Gonchera tried to hide his impatience. The firm of Marshden and Marshden had given the case to Tring because they realised that it was hopeless and only a man of Tring's angry impetuosity would accept the proving of the accused's innocence as a personal crusade which he fought harder and harder as the hopelessness of the fight became more obvious. From the detail of the brief, it was quite clear that Tring must have worked day and night to try to find something in Bill Stemple's favour.

Gonchera addressed the witness. " How many drinks did you have during the course of the evening?"

Gurren answered very quickly. " Not many." His self-satisfied smile said that he was not going to be caught out by that one.

" How many is not many?"

" I can't really remember."

" Surely your mind was clear enough to enable you to give us an estimate now?"

" I wasn't drunk, if that's what you're getting at."

" Did I suggest you were?"

" No. But some of them did."

" Are you talking about those present at the dance?"

" Yes."

" What do you think made them say a thing like that?"

" I don't know."

" Could it be because when ' God Save the Queen ' was played and you tried to stand to attention, you collapsed to the floor?"

Gurren's air of self-satisfaction disappeared. He looked pleadingly at the judge. " I tripped over," he finally muttered.

Gonchera smiled at the jury. They were men and women of the world, his smile said. He sat down and read through part of his instructions yet again. The accused *had* been very upset when drinking with the other four at midnight, but that had been because he had been told the directors knew who had sent the photograph of the Lanfair 850 to the French motoring journal. But that could not be explained because no mention of the source of the two hundred pounds was to be made in court. How much damage would this refusal to tell the truth do to the defence? It was impossible to say. On the face of it, a great deal. But that was to forget that if the jury knew the accused had betrayed his firm—they would never see his act as one of defiance—they would be more likely to think him guilty of murder. A quite illogical reaction, but one which was all too human. Suppose one were willing to accept this risk, how much would the strength of the defence's case be increased by the giving of the true story of the two hundred pounds. Very little, he thought. The rest of the evidence was far too much in the prosecution's favour.

Corinne Hammer gave evidence that she had seen Bill Stemple and Sheila Jones dancing together. In her opinion, their dancing had not been very nice. No, she did not want to explain exactly what she meant, but she certainly did not think people should dance like that. She had not seen Sheila Jones at eleven o'clock.

Gonchera did not cross-examine. Women like Corinne Hammer found any form of embrace obnoxious. The three women on the jury, all of whom looked plumply married, would know that.

" This is a convenient moment for the court to adjourn for the day," said the judge. He advised the jury that they were not to discuss the case with anyone, then bowed to counsel and left the courtroom by the door at the back of the dais.

CHAPTER XI

xxxxxxxxxxxxxxxxxxxxxxxxxxxxxxxxxxxxxxxxxxxxxxxxxx

BILL SAT UP ON the bunk in the cell and stared at the food on a cheap and battered tray. He lit a cigarette. As he inhaled, he coughed.

Before the trial, he had managed to assure himself that at the worst it would be an ordeal he could over-come by firm resolution: but it had proved to be a grim ritual which was steam-rollering him into utter despair. In their many conferences, Tring had talked about fighting on until the truth came out: but how did you fight something impersonal that was infinitely bigger and stronger than you?

Gonchera had tried hard, but had he been twice as successful as in fact he was, his successes would have amounted to nothing. He, Bill, had taken Sheila down to the room where she was killed: he had been with her at a time when medical evidence said she could have died : no one had seen her after 11 o'clock. He knew she had returned to the photography room for her handbag—but who on the jury was going to be " stupid " enough to believe him? It was hopeless already. What would it be when all the police evidence was given? His finger-print had been on the murder weapon : the letters to Heavers had been written on his typewriter . . .

He stubbed out his cigarette. He was innocent, yet only Tring believed it. He corrected himself. One other person knew he was innocent : the murderer. But it was Bill Stemple who was on trial and the jury already knew him to be guilty.

: :   : :

Margaret Stemple pushed her plate to one side. " You've got to eat," said her husband.

" I can't." She picked up her glass and drank, not caring what the wine tasted like.

For the first time, Henry Stemple was seeing his wife trying to gain mental relief from alcohol. The sight hurt him only a little less than did the thought of Bill.

" Why?" she suddenly said.

" Why what?"

" Why did he take her down there?"

" Is anything more obvious?"

" He wasn't short of money. So why in God's name did he take those horrible photos?"

" You know he swears he didn't. He took the girl down there for another purpose."

" Henry, you can't stop me thinking just by making the same denial over and over again. He's going to be found guilty. I want to get used to that so the end of the trial won't shock me."

" He can't have taken those photos. He can't even work a box camera."

" He could have learnt."

" I tell you, he wouldn't do such a thing. He's too decent."

" Who's to say these days what anyone will do?" she answered miserably. She did not seem to realise that she and her husband had changed characters : now it was he who was trying to persuade her of Bill's innocence, against all the evidence, and she who insisted on Bill's guilt.

::   ::

Arthur Gonchera helped himself to more potatoes. " If these were ever new, it was the year before last."

Geraldine Pawley smiled. " It's an odd thing, Arthur, but I've always sworn that the food in this town is even worse than the food in others on the circuit." Her voice was low-pitched and pleasant. Out of court robes, she looked warm-natured and, ironically since she was unmarried, as though she had a large and happy family.

Gonchera helped himself to the remaining peas in the right half of the serving dish. " Kent is a gastronomical desert," he said, with one of the generalisations he so frequently used outside the courtroom.

Geraldine Pawley finished eating. She opened her handbag. " D'you mind if I'm very rude, Arthur, and smoke between courses?"

" Do what you like."

She fitted a cigarette into an ivory holder. " Don't swear too loudly, but Mr. Joshua Tring has just come in."

" Not before the sweet," groaned Gonchera.

Tring walked over to their table, limping more than he usually did. " Mind if I sit down?" he asked, as he did so.

" Have some wine?" asked Gonchera, reluctantly.

Tring upended one of the two unused glasses and filled it. " What's the situation?"

" Bloody awful," replied Gonchera. His answer held a certain ambiguity.

"The evidence from Miss King and the other three wasn't as strong as it might have been."

"Strong enough. Anyway, by the end of the police evidence it won't matter what it was."

"If he didn't kill the girl, someone's lying."

"I should imagine that's true."

Tring ignored the sarcasm. "Then who's lying?"

"If you press me—Stemple."

"You've no . . ."

Gonchera interrupted the other. "You, I, and Miss Pawley, have examined the evidence under a microscope. We've disected it, bisected it, and then started again at the beginning. Remembering that, I'll tell you quite flatly that I'll pay a thousand pounds to charity if I get him off."

"It would help if his own counsel could try to believe in his innocence."

Gonchera gained a sympathetic glance from Geraldine Pawley. He sighed. This argument had completely put him off the sherry trifle that was to come: and it was no relief to know that the sherry trifle would be tasteless. He could judge how Tring felt. Tring was one of those men who could, and sometimes did, identify himself so completely with the case he was handling that he began to feel as if he, himself, were on trial. This explained —some of—Tring's rudeness and apparent naïvety. It could have been an astute move of Marshden to put Tring in charge of the case had there been some facts in favour of the prisoner to uncover. Here, there was none.

       : :   : :

Allenbury called for George Willon to come into the witness-box. The policeman by the second door out of the courtroom opened the door and called for George Willon. From outside, there came a second call for George Willon.

George entered. Staring straight ahead of himself, he

walked forward. He reached the witness-box, climbed the two steps into it, and went forward to the front where the usher was holding up a copy of The New Testament and a card on which was printed the oath.

George took the oath.

Allenbury hitched up his gown on to his shoulders. He rubbed the sides of his over-long nose as he put the preliminary questions, then dropped his right hand to his side. Seconds later, he picked up his spectacles, put them on, and stared for several seconds at the jury. " Mr. Willon, were you friendly with the deceased girl, Miss Sheila Jones?" he asked.

" Yes, sir." George kept fidgeting. Because of this, his badly fitting coat slipped down his back until the top of it was below his shirt collar.

" Exactly how friendly were you?"

" I wanted to marry her."

" Did you ever ask her to marry you?"

" Several times," replied George, in a low voice.

" With what result?"

" She said we must wait."

" For what?"

" I was hoping to get a reasonable rise in pay. Sheila rather liked . . . What I mean is . . ." He became silent.

" Take your time, Mr. Willon."

When next he spoke, George did so as quickly as possible. " She was rather fond of expensive things."

" Did you see her on the night of the dance?"

" I met her beforehand and we had a drink or two. After that, we went to the dance."

" In fact, you partnered her there?"

" Yes, sir."

" What happened at the dance?"

" She went off with him." George looked quickly at Bill in the dock.

" For how long?"

" The rest of the evening."

" Did you see them again?"

" During supper and when they were playing tombola."

" How did you feel about what was happening?"

" I . . . I felt rotten. He never intended to marry her, but he knew she liked the money he spent on her and his position. It wasn't her fault, it really wasn't. She just thought it was all so important."

There was some surprise that Allenbury had allowed the witness to speak as he had. There was more surprise when Allenbury said slowly: " Were you so jealous that, in fact, you killed Miss Jones?"

" No." George's voice rose. " I couldn't have done that. Can't you understand, I loved her. I couldn't."

Allenbury slowly removed his spectacles and put them down on top of his copy of Archbold. " Thank you for removing that possibility from the minds of the jury. Now, let's study in more detail the events of that terrible evening."

: :   : :

Gonchera, as he cross-examined George, admitted to himself that his learned friend had stolen most of his thunder. As the jury had known from the beginning, George was the only other obvious possible suspect because he was the jealous lover. But by allowing George openly to express his jealousy in his examination-in-chief together with his denial of being the murderer, Allenbury had made certain that any further questioning along these lines by Gonchera would only cause resentment in the minds of the jury.

" You have told us, Mr. Willon, that after dancing with you for some time, the deceased danced with Mr. Stemple?"

" Yes."

" And that they had supper together. Had you no idea they would be having supper together?"

" I thought she'd be having it with me."

" Did you consider joining them?"

" It was obvious they didn't want me."

" You spoke to them just before they went into the room in which the tombola was being held, didn't you?"

" Yes."

" What did you say?"

" I asked her if she'd dance with me, but she refused."

" Was it then that you told her you had arranged transport home for the two of you and she replied she already had a car to take her?"

" I said Reg Trayner would drive us back home, but she refused."

" And she mentioned this other car?"

" No."

" Are you certain? The accused will say that she did."

George shook his head. When told he must answer aloud, he said, " No," in what was almost a shout.

" Mr. Willon, if the deceased did say this, you must . . ."

The judge intervened. " The witness has denied that she did, Mr. Gonchera."

" Quite so, my Lord."

" Have you any proof to the contrary?"

" The accused, my Lord, will say . . ."

" Other than what the accused may, or may not, say, Mr. Gonchera?" The judge's tone of voice, which would never appear in the shorthand report of the case, said clearly what weight he would expect could be attached to the accused's claim.

Gonchera spoke impatiently. " No, my Lord, no other proof. But in a matter like this . . ."

" Then you will kindly not press the witness further on this point."

Gonchera faced the witness again. " When did you next see the accused after the time in the tombola room?"

" When he was drinking in the annex with the others."

" Who were these others?"

" Miss King, Carthwright, Gurren, and Vigen."

" Did you see him after this?"

" Not that night."

" Mr. Willon, is it not a fact that you saw him down in the basement?"

" I didn't go near the basement."

" Are you telling the truth?"

" I didn't go down there."

Gonchera spoke quite slowly, emphasising nearly every word. " The accused will testify that when he and Miss Jones left the photography room, she suddenly said that she thought she had seen you farther along the passage."

" That's impossible."

" Why should she have said that if she did not see you?"

" Perhaps she didn't say it."

" You'll kindly answer the question and nothing more."

Mr. Justice Waring put his pencil down on his notebook. " Do you object, then, Mr. Gonchera, to the witness's suggestion?"

" I most certainly do, my Lord."

" Why?"

" He is not entitled to make it."

" Very strictly speaking, perhaps not. You would rather that the suggestion had not been put before the jury?"

" It is not for this witness to comment on the evidence, my Lord," said Gonchera, with dogged perseverance.

" But if he had not done so, I feel certain your learned friend would have."

Gonchera was silent. The judge was well known for the way in which he would expose the weaknesses of the case for either the prosecution or the defence.

Gonchera stared at the witness. If only he had been given something with which to fight, he thought bitterly. But to fight just for the sake of fighting, and without ammunition, was to alienate the jury. George Willon had given his evidence with the simple directness that meant—lacking contrary evidence—it would be believed.

He reluctantly continued his cross-examination.

: :   : :

The police evidence took up the remainder of the day.

Photographs of the dead girl's body were passed to the jury. The finding of the tripod, the camera, and the handbag, were described. The pathologist placed the time of death between 11.30 and 1.30 and reluctantly admitted that these times agreed with those suggested by the police doctor : he also gave evidence about the thin skull. A finger-print expert proved, by demonstrating twelve similar characteristics in each case, that the finger-prints on the tripod were those of the prisoner. Detective Inspector Shute was over two hours in the witness-box as he detailed every move of the investigation : the cross-examination of him was completely ineffective, as Gonchera would have been the first to admit. Witnesses proved that the envelope containing the fifty pounds found in the dead girl's handbag had been traced to Heavers, that the police had been given two letters by Heavers, and that these had been typed on a typewriter in the prisoner's office on paper exactly similar to that used by him. Evidence was given that on June 9th two hundred pounds in one-pound notes had been paid into the accused's account.

Gonchera cross-examined the bank cashier.

"You have testified that there can be no doubt that this sum was paid in in one-pound notes. Can you remember their condition?"

" No, sir."

" You cannot tell us whether they were new or old?"

" No, sir."

" Have you examined Mr. William Stemple's account in order to check whether there were other large payments in in cash over the past year and a half?"

" Yes, sir."

" What did you find?"

" There were no such payments."

" Did you also search this account for any payments by cheque, the cheques to be drawn on Mr. Heavers's bank?"

" Yes, sir."

" Were there any such?"

" No, sir. None."

That marked the end of the day's hearing.

: :   : :

At the beginning of the third day of the trial, when the name of Heavers was called, there was a hasty whispered conference between prosecuting counsel and a uniformed police superintendent. After this, Allenbury addressed the Bench. " My Lord, I regret to have to inform the court that this witness died during the night at his own hand."

Shute, sitting at the end of one of the benches, shivered. He remembered Mrs. Heavers, the Norwegian girl, and the peace of the tastefully decorated house. He knew that he was going to feel responsible, in part, for that man's death no matter that he was not to blame. He silently cursed the fact that no crime was ever contained within itself: always, the bitter ripples spread outwards.

Allenbury spoke. " I should like, my Lord, to call a witness to prove the death of Mr. Heavers with a view to having his deposition read at this trial."

The judge agreed.

Gonchera stood up. " My Lord, the Criminal Justice Act lays down the steps necessary before the deposition of a dead man may be read in court and, of course, my learned friend is perfectly correct in the course he wishes to adopt. But I must point out that, as the court will understand, a full cross-examination of Mr. Heavers was not carried out at the preliminary hearing. Indeed, the accused was represented only by his solicitor who very rightly restricted his questioning to a minimum."

Mr. Justice Waring picked out a thick text book from the small row of books on his right. In the ensuing three minutes, he read through certain passages, to the accompaniment of an increasing noise from the public which ceased as soon as he spoke. " The deposition will be read, Mr. Gonchera. After that, it might perhaps be fairest if you point out, very briefly, what questions you would have put to the witness had he appeared in court this morning."

Allenbury called the police superintendent into the witness-box. The superintendent took the oath and gave evidence that Heavers had committed suicide at some time of the night and that he, the superintendent, had viewed the body. He went on to testify that he had been in court when the deposition was taken before magistrates in the presence of the accused and that the accused, or his solicitor, had had the opportunity to cross-examine the witness.

The deposition, a record of the evidence that Heavers had given in the magistrates' court, was then read out.

Gonchera.addressed the Bench. " My Lord, we have heard a reasonably full account of the dead man's activities, the way in which he conducted his obnoxious trade, and the manner in which he first came to be supplied with photographs of the dead girl. We have already heard from Detective Inspector Shute that he was handed the two letters by Mr. Heavers and we have heard what happened to these two letters. I should now briefly like to mention the dates on which Heavers left money in an envelope in the hollow of the tree in Hyde Park. Those dates are September fourteenth, November second, December fourteenth, of last year, and January fourth, February eighth, March twenty-eighth, April twenty-fifth, May sixteenth, and June sixth, of this year. The prosecution pointed out, at some length I might add, that all these days were Saturdays, a day, of course, when no work was done in the publicity department of Lanfairs. But had I been cross-examining Heavers here and now I would have asked him whether he was quite certain those dates are the correct ones and on his answering in the affirmative I would have proved that my client was in Jersey before, during, and after September fourteenth and therefore could not have been the person who collected a hundred and fifty-pounds from the tree. I would also have made him confirm that on June sixth he left only a hundred and fifty pounds in the tree: of which, of course, we must presume fifty pounds was the fifty pounds found in the dead girl's handbag."

The judge spoke with only mild sarcasm. " I'm quite certain, Mr. Gonchera, the jury will have appreciated the way in which you would have put these points had the witness been alive to-day. Indeed, the way in which you have put them now that we have been advised of his death."

Gonchera bowed and sat down. He was prepared to say that Heavers's death had proved advantageous to the defence since there could be no re-examination on what he had just said.

: :   : :

Bill was in the dock. Fear had become panic, panic had seesawed to desperate hope which, in turn, had plunged down to complete despair.

At the beginning of the trial he had presumed he enjoyed the benefits of innocence: now that the trial was nearly over he knew he was considered to bear the burden of guilt. Before, in his bitterest moments, he had been content to believe that, fairy-tale-like, at the last moment his innocence would be proved: now, he knew that there was to be no fairy-tale ending. Yet, still the instinct of self-preservation forced him on. Still, he desperately tried to show the nine men and three women of the jury that, no matter what it seemed like, he had not killed her. Still, the cry of "But I'm innocent" thundered in his mind.

"Mr. Stemple," said Gonchera, in the middle of his examination-in-chief, "are you quite certain you left Miss Sheila Jones at the head of the basement stairs?"

"She said she'd forgotten her handbag. That's the last time I ever saw her."

"Were you aware that she was posing for pornographic pictures?"

"No."

"You had no inkling of that fact?"

"No."

"What were your feelings when you learned the truth?"

"I still can't believe it."

"Why not?"

"She was too . . . too prudish."

Gonchera swore silently. Why had the witness chosen a word, however naturally it fitted the context, which would almost certainly remind the jury of his attempts to seduce her? "Have you entered any of the London parks in the past eighteen months?" he asked, quickly altering the line of questioning.

"I don't often go to London. When I do, I don't go near the parks."

" Have you any idea when was the last time you were in Hyde Park?"

" I haven't."

" Will you please tell the jury where you were on September fourteenth of last year?"

" On holiday in Jersey."

" During what dates were you there?"

" I went on the ninth and came back on the twentieth."

Gonchera addressed the jury. " Members of the jury, I shall be calling witnesses to show that the accused was in Jersey during the days he says he was and that he was in Jersey for the whole of the fourteenth." He turned back and faced the witness-box. " Were you in London on any of the other dates on which money was left by Heavers in Hyde Park?"

" No."

" Can you prove you were not?"

" I can't. But I never went up to London . . ."

" Quite so." Very quickly, Gonchera stopped Bill's words. " On the eleventh of June you deposited two hundred pounds in cash in your bank. Is that correct?"

" Yes."

" Where did the money come from?"

" I won it at Folkestone races."

" On one race?"

" I lost on one and won on three."

" Have you at any other time deposited large sums in cash in your bank?"

" No."

" You have never regularly deposited sums in cash, as you would have done had you been in receipt of the money the prosecution claims you were?"

Allenbury loudly muttered an objection to the form of the question.

" No," answered Bill.

" Who used the typewriter in your office?"

" I did, and any of the typists who worked for me."

" Anybody else?"

" Not to my knowledge."

" Would you have known had anyone else used it?"

" No, because I wasn't there all the time. Anyone in the building could have used it when I wasn't around."

" Did you type the two letters about which we have heard so much?"

" I did not."

Allenbury's cross-examination, which followed half an hour later, was long and thorough. Too long and too thorough, was the verdict of many.

"You went down to the photography room at about eleven o'clock?"

Bill's face was pale. He looked very tired. " Yes."

" To do what?"

Everyone knew what, thought Bill wildly. Why make him say it aloud. " To be on our own."

" Why did you want to be on your own?"

" To . . . to neck."

" And did you?"

" Yes."

" Were you successful?"

" Nothing happened, if that's what you mean."

" I suppose that annoyed you?"

" No," he muttered.

" Speak up, please."

" I said it didn't annoy me."

" Not? Then you are used to dealing with women who fail to succumb to your charms? Tell me, Mr. Stemple, wasn't it at this time that you claim you picked up the tripod?"

" I took it off the couch at the beginning."

" The jury may find it difficult to believe that the tripod was ever on the couch in the first place. Mr.

Willon, who is in charge of the room, says it has never been there to his knowledge."

" I tell you, it was there."

" Or is this part of the story made up by you in order to explain how your finger-prints came to be on the murder weapon?"

" I've told you exactly what happened." Because Bill was desperately trying to keep control of his feelings, his voice sounded almost sullen.

Allenbury shrugged his shoulders. " Let's move on in time. You claim you left the photography room with Miss Jones?"

" I did leave with her."

" And you both reached the head of the stairs before she said she had forgotten the handbag?"

" Yes."

" Why didn't you go back and get it for her? Wouldn't that have been the gentlemanly thing to have done?"

" I offered to."

" But, of course, she refused?"

" She said she'd get it and I wasn't to wait for her."

" Did she say why not?"

" Because someone else was taking her home."

" That, presumably, is the same someone you claim she mentioned to Mr. Willon?"

" Yes."

" Didn't this surprise you?"

" In a way."

" Did you not want to know from her who it was?"

" No."

" What was the matter? Were you too furious at having failed to seduce her?"

Bill struggled to find some way of explaining what had happened, and failed.

Allenbury leaned forward and raised his voice slightly. " Isn't all this one long lie? Isn't it the truth that you reached the top of the basement stairs on your own for the very simple reason that Sheila Jones was lying dead on the floor of the photography room?"

"I didn't kill her. I swear I didn't. I wasn't taking those photographs. You've got to believe me . . ."

"No, Mr. Stemple, it is the jury you have to ask to believe you." Allenbury picked up his glasses and played with them, swinging them round in his hands. "If she returned for her handbag, as you claim, presumably she returned upstairs when she had it?"

"I don't know."

"Surely that's the logical thing to suppose? A girl says 'I've forgotten my handbag, I must go and get it.' Does that not presuppose that when she has it she will continue on towards wherever she was going? In other words, to the dance floor? Doesn't it?"

"She must have waited in the photography room."

"No one saw her alive after you and she went down to the photography room."

"She must have waited there for whoever was taking the photographs."

"Nobody," repeated Allenbury, "saw her again. Alive."

        : :   : :

Because witnesses for the defence as to facts had been called, Gonchera delivered his closing speech before Allenbury. With all the skill at his command, he repeated Bill's story and tried to show how Bill had been caught in a web of incriminating circumstances because of an act which only a Victorian moralist could, or would, condemn.

". . . What is the motive supposed to be?" he demanded. "The prosecution say he killed her because of an argument over the photographs that he was taking—and let me remind you here that the camera has never been traced within a thousand miles of his

I

possession. What argument? The photographs taken show that Miss Jones was posing happily. The prosecution says that he may have attacked her for obvious reasons and he killed her. Let us not be mealy-mouthed : their suggestion is that he was trying to rape her. But, members of the jury, the medical evidence is that she was not interfered with, sexually, in any way whatsoever. So what possible motive can there have been?

"Let me point out another very great discrepancy in the prosecution's case. Money. The photographs were being taken because this sordid trade is an extremely profitable one. Records show that during the time Miss Jones posed for these photographs she banked four hundred pounds. If she received fifty pounds for each photograph accepted—remember, only one was chosen out of each series taken—and you take note of the fifty pounds in her bag, then this sum of money exactly corresponds with the nine dates on which the dead man, Heavers, testified that he left money in the tree in Hyde Park. That leaves nine hundred pounds for the person who sent the photographs to Heavers. Where is this money? The prosecution keeps harping on the two hundred pounds the accused banked on June ninth. But that is only two, not nine, hundred. And remember this very well, although the full sum was paid out in the beginning of June and fifty pounds of this was given to the dead girl, two hundred was paid by my client into his bank and this is twice the sum he could have received from Heavers.

"We were given the dates on which the money was left in Hyde Park. The prosecution contends that my client collected this money. But, as you have heard, on the first named date he was in Jersey and could not possibly have collected the money.

"Members of the jury, I ask you to consider these facts and then come to the obvious conclusion. William Stemple was not, and could not be, the photographer.

There is a second person in this case, the person who murdered Sheila Jones . . ."

: :   : :

As was to be expected, Allenbury's closing speech was so detailed and so prolonged that to his listeners it seemed as if he dotted every i twice and crossed every t at least four times.

" . . . My learned friend has pointed out what he is pleased to term two inconsistencies. He has made great play with them. Were I a man to labour a point, I might add that he has undoubtedly made great play of them because he has so little else to play with.

" Shall we examine these points calmly? On September fourteenth, one hundred and fifty pounds was left in the tree in Hyde Park. On this date, the prisoner was in Jersey. Naturally, if the date is correct, the prisoner could not have collected the money. That, says the defence, proves he is not the photographer and did not murder Sheila Jones. Shall we introduce the light of logic into the murk of this reasoning? Suppose Heavers was wrong in the first date he gave? After all, he was keeping a record of events solely for himself. He could very easily have been a week out and it would not matter a fig. Let me put it in another way. Had the accused been able to show that he was clearly unable to collect the money on any of the dates given, then it would have been ridiculous of me to suggest that all the dates were wrong and I would have agreed that it had not been he who collected the money. However, shall we remember—as the defence did not—that the prisoner could easily have delegated someone else to collect the money? I put that to you simply and solely to show that it is totally incorrect to claim that if the prisoner did not collect the money he could not have been the murderer.

" Members of the jury, the defence made the somewhat startling statement that because the prisoner paid in two hundred pounds when he had only received a hundred had he been the photographer, this must prove the two hundred pounds had nothing to do with the payment on June sixth. Are we, then, not to be allowed to understand that the lesser may be contained within the greater? Are we not to suppose that he could have been paid for two photographs at once? Would you then be worried because only fifty pounds was found in the dead girl's handbag and not a hundred? Let us examine the various permutations . . ."

And Allenbury proceeded to examine the permutations : every single one of them.

: :   : :

Mr. Justice Waring's summing-up was relatively short, lucid, and in no way favourable to the accused.

" . . . The two letters were written on the typewriter in his room, on paper exactly similar to that which he used. It must be, therefore, that either he, or someone who had easy access to his office, wrote those two letters. The defence suggested it might have been the dead girl herself, but that is to credit her with the major part in this unpleasant undertaking and if that were so, I venture to suggest she would have reaped the major portion of the rewards. Members of the jury, you will decide whether you can believe the defence's submission or whether you believe the prosecution's. You will place this piece of evidence in line with all the other evidence.

" I want you, if you will, to think deeply on what significance you attach to the extraordinary precautions which were taken to make certain Mr. Heavers did not meet the person who was collecting the money. Counsel referred to these precautions as suggesting the setting of some espionage affair and this was an apt picture. You may well think the precautions were taken because the person who was selling the photographs was in a position, social and in the business world, in which he dreaded exposure.

" Members of the jury, few murders are not circumstantial because few murders are committed in front of witnesses. The facts of the killing, and you must not forget the alternative verdict of manslaughter which you are at liberty to bring in should you find the accused killed the deceased but did not do so with express or implied malice, have to be implied from the circumstances.

" Miss Jones was killed by a blow on her head, delivered with a wooden camera tripod. On this tripod was a finger-print proved to be that of the accused . . ."

: :   : :

The jury returned into court. After a wait of only seconds, the judge hurried in and crossed to his desk.

Bill dug his fingers into the palms of his hands. He could feel sweat trickling down the back of his neck.

The clerk of the court asked the jury if they had arrived at a verdict.

There was surprise when it was discovered the jury had returned to court merely to seek advice.

" We can't agree," said the foreman.

The judge looked up at the electric clock. " You have not been considering the verdict for very long. Would it not be best to return to the jury-room and examine the matter further? As you will know, your verdict must be the verdict of all of you and if you disagree to the extent of there being no hope of agreement it will become my duty to discharge you, but such action will only be taken when there is very obviously no hope of your ever reaching agreement."

The foreman of the jury was a large, well-rounded man who looked what he was, a prosperous farmer. " Eleven of us say guilty, but he keeps . . ." He had, without conscious volition, turned and was staring at the last man in the front row.

" We can't have that," said the judge sharply. " This court is not allowed to know the state of voting. You will retire again and see whether further consideration on the part of all of you will lead to a verdict."

: :   : :

The jury returned as the setting sun was sending a shaft of pale sunlight through the raised glass fanlight.

The clerk of the court spoke to the foreman of the jury.

" Guilty," replied the foreman.

CHAPTER XII

✕✕

WITH FEW EXCEPTIONS, those who worked in Publicity had subconsciously expected the murder and the trial to have a far greater effect than they did. In the event, the staff found they had discussed the case so often amongst themselves, and Bill Stemple had been so obviously guilty from the very beginning, that the actual result had proved to be an anti-climax.

Parry finished dictating a letter. " Send it off air mail."

" Yes, Mr. Parry," answered Corinne Hammer. She closed her notebook. " Have you the address, please?"

He looked at her in astonishment. " It's surely in the file for Israel?"

" Of course," she said, in a low voice. Her heavy face settled into ugly lines of distress. " I . . . I keep thinking about it, Mr. Parry."

" What?"

" That there are people who enjoy those photographs. It's terrible."

" Didn't someone once say that human nature was both sides of a mirror so that every emotion was reflected in reverse?"

" What's . . . what's going to happen to him?"

Parry shook his head. " Let's forget it, Miss Hammer. It doesn't do to get morbid."

" But I . . ."

" Would you please get that letter done?"

She was shocked by the sharp tone of his voice. She slowly stood up, stared at him in bewilderment, then left.

After she had gone, Parry reached over to the intercom and depressed a switch.

" Press room."

" Is that you, Carthwright?"

" None other."

" Will you come and have a word with me, please." Parry picked up a pencil and fiddled with it. When the door opened and Carthwright entered, he leaned back in his chair.

" What a day!" said Carthwright, as he walked up to the desk. " Makes me nostalgic for Bondi, the surf, and all those lovely sheilas in bikinis."

Parry believed that the unspoken stress on the virility of such a scene was there for his benefit. " The English weather is always unpredictable," he replied, with crushing triteness. " Will you sit down."

Carthwright lounged back in the chair. He was wearing sports coat and grey flannels, although regulation dress for the office was a suit.

Parry suddenly realised he was fiddling with the pencil and he dropped it. " I've just seen Mr. Andover."

" How is the old bastard?"

" I think you ought not to . . ." Parry did not finish the sentence. " I'm very sorry, Mr. Carthwright, but it seems probable that Mr. Stemple's position will be filled by someone from outside."

" I can imagine."

" I insisted you were perfectly capable of carrying out the job, but he wishes it otherwise."

"Him and me are like that," said Carthwright. He held out his right hand with middle finger across the top of his forefinger. "The trouble is, we can't agree who's on top."

"I'm sorry."

Carthwright grinned. "Hell! Tie me to an executive position and you'd choke the life out of me."

Parry did not try to hide his relief at the fact that the interview was proceeding so smoothly. "I'd be grateful if you'd carry on as you are until they appoint someone else. It may take time."

"Sure."

Parry coughed, to show that the matter they had been discussing was now over and done with. "Have you had any ideas on producing something to counteract all the adverse publicity?"

"No, and I don't reckon it's needed. You Pommies like your murders so much everyone will be falling over their necks to buy a Lanfair Fifteen Thousand, de luxe, all the same as Bill had."

A few minutes later, Carthwright returned to what had been Bill's office. Janet was sitting behind the desk. When she saw his expression, she said: "What's up?"

"The bastards."

"Who?"

"The whole shower." He went round and stood behind her chair. For a while there was silence, then Janet giggled. Eventually, she stood up. He sat down in his chair.

"They're bringing in someone from outside to take over this job."

"But you've done so well." She suddenly realised something. "That means you won't have an office of your own any more."

"That's it."

"But how am I going to live?"

His voice became angry. "It's those fat-arsed directors trying to get one of their chosen little boys a job. It's no wonder this country's on the rocks—you've all forgotten what honest sex is about."

Janet pouted. " I don't think it's fair to say that to me."

:   :   :   :

Henry Stemple watched the tractor move very slowly along the top of the bank. Its cab was fitted with safety bars, a necessary precaution in view of the gradient of the slope. He looked past the tractor and up at the hills. To the right, a clump of trees on the skyline had the appearance of a liner's foredeck : fifty yards along were three poplars which provided the funnels. He desperately wished he and Margaret could leave the farm and go for a long sea cruise. They had always promised themselves they would have one one day, but had never found either the time or the money. Yet, he thought bitterly, even had they been able to go immediately, would it have eased her mental suffering?

The tractor came to a halt on a relatively flat section of ground and the driver switched off the engine. He walked down the slope. " One-thirty, then," he said, as he passed Henry Stemple.

Henry Stemple nodded. His men had tried to show their sympathy by not making a single reference to the trial or its result, yet sometimes he found their silence harder to bear than an open interest. He turned and went through the field to the yard and the cinder path which brought him to the back door of the house.

Margaret Stemple was in the kitchen, frying potatoes. " Lunch is nearly ready."

He stared out of the window. When next he looked at her, she was crying. He crossed and put his hand on her shoulder. " Stop thinking about it."

She shook her head. " How can I?" she said, with the anger of deep grief. " Everything reminds me of him. I never lay the table for more than two. When I took the joint from the refrigerator I was surprised there was so much left, until I remembered. Henry, isn't there anything we can do?"

" Such as?"

" If I knew, I wouldn't ask. He's your son as much as mine. Suppose you start thinking about him?"

" D'you think I haven't been?"

She turned and pressed herself against him. " I didn't mean that," she whispered.

: :   : :

Marshden stood in his office with his back to the gas fire. His silver-grey hair was exactly parted, his tie was precisely knotted, and his black coat and striped trousers could have come back from the cleaners that day. In direct contrast, Joshua Tring looked as if he had just completed eighteen windy holes at Sandwich.

" I don't see really you can do anything," said Marshden, in his slow, deep, voice.

" Appeal, of course."

" Which on your own admission won't get you very far. You've a right of appeal on law, but there certainly wasn't much of that. You'll have to get the leave of the Court of Appeal or a certificate from Waring that it's a fit case for appeal if you try on the facts. Can you see old Waring being sympathetic?"

" All that doesn't matter . . ."

" Unfortunately, Joshua, it most certainly does."

" The man happens to be innocent."

Marshden walked slowly over to his desk and sat down. " What makes you so certain?"

" A guilty man couldn't have talked to me the way he did."

" I suppose it's no good, Joshua, giving you my usual little lecture on the dangers to the lawyer of instinctive emotionalism?"

" No bloody use whatsoever."

" All right, then. What about the evidence?"

" That's the strongest point in his favour. It's so overwhelmingly against him."

" I doubt you'll find anyone but yourself to see the logic of that."

" Logic? Of course it's logical. Look. If he'd killed the girl, don't you think he'd have made damn' sure he covered himself as far as he could? Yet he didn't begin to try."

" You're introducing a new maxim into our law, then? The greater the evidence against a man, the greater must be the presumption of his innocence?"

" You know what I mean."

" Do I?" Marshden sighed. " Suppose I agree it wasn't Stemple. Who was it then? The chap who worked in the photography department?"

Tring helped himself to a cigarette from the opened packet on the desk. " George Willon is the natural. He wanted to marry the girl and was jealous of Bill because Bill had more money and was therefore apparently getting further with her. But the police checked on him as hard as they checked on Stemple. Apart from a minute or two towards the end of the evening, all his time's accounted for. That means it could just conceivably have been he if any evidence fitted in with his guilt, but it doesn't. Gonchera and I went over and over his evidence to see whether to make his possible guilt our line of attack and it just wasn't feasible. Apart from anything else, if he'd been making a hundred quid a photo, he'd have been taking her out to all those expensive restaurants."

" Very well, Willon cannot be suspected." Marshden opened one of the top drawers of his desk and brought out a cigar in its own container. He unscrewed the metal cap, slid the cigar out, and pierced the end. " Whom else do you suspect?" He lit the cigar.

" Anyone."

" Motive?"

" What the hell was Bill's motive supposed to be? What really was the motive? The photographer was getting along very smoothly, judging by the photos, and then he suddenly ups and kills the girl. Why? I'm telling you, Edward, that's the crux of the matter."

" Stemple got too excited."

" Where were the inevitable bruises?"

" All these questions were put to the jury, Joshua."

" Who were ignorant enough to ignore them." Tring began to pace the floor, limping slightly. " Or else were blinded by their priggish abhorrence of what was going on."

" But you're not priggish?"

Tring stopped by the desk. He spoke belligerently. " I'm telling you that Stemple is innocent."

" You're insisting on telling me you believe him innocent on absolutely no evidence whatsoever and mainly probably because everyone else says he's guilty." Marshden held the cigar in front of him and watched the spiralling smoke. " I'd give a hell of a lot to be able to help Bill Stemple, even if I don't reckon he's as good a man as his father, but we've done all we can."

" I'm going to appeal."

" One usually does, in a case of murder. But it's a formality."

" Is it?" snapped Tring. " Not if you make certain it isn't."

Marshden's voice suddenly expressed worry. " For God's sake, Joshua, don't go and do something damn' silly."

" I'll do something very damn' silly—if only I can find it to do."

: :   : :

Detective Superintendent Easdale walked into Shute's

room at Leamarsh police station without knocking on the door.

Shute, who had been reading through reports from his detective constables, looked up. " 'Morning, sir."

" The A.C.C. told me to say he was quite pleased with your handling of the Stemple case."

Shute thought it must have upset Easdale quite a lot to have to deliver so complimentary a message from the assistant chief constable.

As if to prove the truth of the D.I.'s thoughts, Easdale began to complain. " I've been looking through the records. They don't make pretty reading."

" No, sir?"

" Far too many unsolved crimes, most of 'em petty ones which you blokes don't think are worthy of investigating. What none of you bother to realise is that successful crime prevention and detection necessitates . . ."

It was not the first time Shute had heard those words. He allowed his mind to wander. The first murder case in U division for a number of years was over and done with and the murderer was in prison. Yet he, Shute, still felt puzzled by some aspects of it. Take the girl. Everyone said what a nice girl she had been : many went further and called her a prude. How could their estimates of her character match up to the realities of her behaviour?

" Are you listening to me?" demanded Easdale angrily.

" Of course, sir."

" It doesn't seem like it."

" Why not?"

" I asked you how many acts of vandalism had been reported in this division in the past month?"

" Fourteen, sir," replied Shute, giving the first figure that suggested itself. " The street lights by the memorial recreation ground are an irresistible target."

" Why haven't you stopped these incidents?"

How do you stop snow falling, wondered Shute?

: :   : :

For a man who was usually " agin " authority, Joshua
Tring had a strangely unbending veneration for what
he considered to be the verities of life. It was this
veneration which had led him into open conflict with
the German guards: it was this veneration which was
driving him on to continue the fight on behalf of
William Stemple.

William Stemple had to be helped for many reasons.
Everyone had said he was guilty before the trial had
been held: that was the baying of the masses, an evil
to be fought at all costs. The evidence was overwhelmingly against him, which left him the underdog. And,
more than anything else, he, Tring, believed Bill innocent
with the kind of blind intensity which scorned logic. So
what in the hell was he going to do to help an innocent
man who had been found guilty and condemned to life
imprisonment?

Catherine, Tring's wife, was a very happy woman.
She understood the impetuous, and to others illogical,
character of her husband and had so learned to live
with it that there had never been a moment when she
regretted marrying him. She spoke to him as he paced
the floor behind the dining-room table. " Your chop's
getting cold, Jos."

" Is it?" he asked, without interest.

She watched him cross to the window recess and pick
up one of the law books that was there.

" A man ought to be given the absolute right to appeal
and not have to get the say-so of some goddam judge,"
he said angrily.

She began to eat her chop. When Joshua insulted the
Bench, she knew he was terribly worried.

" The appeal is only of right if it solely concerns
law. Good God! Most murder cases don't provide
enough law to tax the brains of first-year students."

He shut the book with a bang and put it down. Then he picked it up again and began to read through the index.

She stopped eating as she thought she heard a call from one of their two children.

" How d'you force the truth out of people?" he demanded.

" What is truth?" she asked.

" ' " What is truth?" said jesting Pilate: and would not stay for an answer '." He sat down on the window seat. " The truth is simple: he is not the murderer. But who is going to stay for that answer?"

" He could be a very clever liar, Jos."

" He could be. But I know he isn't."

" Would you come and eat your chop?"

" What chop?"

" It's been on your plate for over five minutes now and soon it'll be too cold to be eatable."

He nodded and crossed to his seat. He ate in silence.

" You can have ice cream or chocolate blancmange?" she said.

" Whichever you like." He ran his fingers through his hair. " Someone must have lied during the trial if Stemple's innocent. At some stage of the trial, the murderer must have had to lie. Isn't that so?"

" Probably. We'll have the blancmange, then, with the rest of the cream my mother gave us."

" One lie would be enough for us. People don't lie unless they have reason."

She stood and collected up the dirty plates.

" But how in the hell do you get anywhere? How do you appeal when there aren't any grounds for appeal? Yet we've got to find the liar." He began to fiddle with the small piece of bread remaining on his side plate. " The law's all wrong. What right has it to bar an innocent man from . . ." He stared at her. " Good God!" He stood up so suddenly and unexpectedly

that she was startled to the point where she almost dropped the plates. She watched him rush across to the
window seat and begin to search through one of the
text books with an impatience that resulted in one of
the pages being torn.

She carried the plates out into the kitchen. He made
life difficult, at times, but she was very sensible and was
thankful that that was so.

: :   : :

At one time, Ashford had been a reasonably attractive
market town, but the decision to turn it into an over-
spill for London and to attract industry to it made certain that all attraction was slowly throttled into extinction.

Green lived in one of the new houses, whose qualities
could have been used as a visual warning to tyro
architects, which were spreading across and burying
the green fields like some obscene acne. He was an
enthusiastic gardener who, since his wife's death, had
interested himself in the culture of orchids. He was
in the greenhouse, adjusting the rush shades, when he
heard the front-door bell chime. He hurried through
the house and opened the front door. He saw a man
whom he thought he recognised, yet could not place.

"May I have a word with you, Mr. Green?" asked
Tring.

"Well, yes, I suppose so."

"I won't bother you for long." Tring entered the
house. He was risking his professional future and that
made him nervous : not because of what could happen
to him, but because of what could happen to his family.
Showing his bewilderment, Green held open the door
of the sitting-room. "You were on the jury of the
Stemple case," said Tring, as soon as they were both
inside.

Green suddenly realised who his caller was. "And you
were for him."

Tring put his hand in his coat pocket. He touched

the rabbit's foot, an act that came straight from his childhood. "You were the juryman who thought him innocent until the pressure grew."

Green looked embarrassed. "I tried. I kept on arguing, but they wouldn't listen to what I was saying. They were all so certain. After the judge had said we had to return to the room to try to reach a decision, they all went for me. Said I must be a fool to think he could be innocent."

"And you let them persuade you?" Tring could not understand that.

"I tell you, it was one against eleven. And the ladies were worse than any of 'em."

"Do you still think he's innocent?"

"I never said he was completely innocent, like. He must have been mixed up in it, or they wouldn't have tried him, would they? But I just don't think it was like the prosecution said."

"He did not kill her."

Green shifted his weight from one foot to the other, and then back again.

Tring spoke loudly. "Are you willing to help him prove his innocence?"

"I don't know what you're talking about."

"Are you willing to help him prove he didn't kill the girl?"

"I don't know. Well, I mean, the trial's over. What can I do?"

"Exactly as I tell you."

Green's expression changed. "Here. You're not acting right, are you? You're trying to do something that shouldn't be done."

"The right thing to do is to see that justice is done."

Green spoke with nervous haste. "I'm not mucking around and that's straight. I did all I could for him and if that wasn't good enough it's too bad."

"Don't you want to ease your conscience?"

" My what?"

" Your conscience. It keeps kicking you where it hurts, doesn't it? You let the other eleven shout you down. You swore to try the case according to your own conscience, but you tried it by those of the other eleven."

Green moved his hands in a mute gesture of bitter mental conflict.

" If the truth comes out, you'll have squared yourself. Mr. Green, I'm asking you to do no more than make a journey to London. The very worst that could happen to you will be a mild rebuke from the Bench."

" I don't . . ." Green longed to be able to refuse whatever it was he was about to be forced to do, but the other's personality and his own conscience were too strong for him. He was a coward who was not coward enough.

    : :   : :

From the moment of the verdict, Bill's mind had been shocked to the point where it partially refused to admit the facts that were fed into it. Yet even then, he subconsciously knew that soon he would have to live with reality and that was why when he was told his lawyer wanted to see him, he cursed wildly. Reality was being forced on him.

He was escorted to the conference room by a warder who smelled of hair cream. Joshua Tring shook hands. As Bill sat down, Tring took a packet of cigarettes from his pocket and put them on the table. " Make hay while the sun shines." He picked up one of the wooden chairs and turned it so that the seat was towards him, then he rested his right foot on it. " We've got to decide whether to appeal."

Bill lit a cigarette. " Appeal?" he said harshly.

" Have you got the guts to fight?"

" Guts? Where do they come into it? The last time I saw Sheila was from the top of the stairs and that's the truth. Yet now I'm a murderer and the truth is a lie."

"Moaning won't get you very far."

Bill stared at Tring and suddenly hated this long, lean, man whose expression always seemed to be telling the world to go to hell.

Tring moved his foot and then sat down. "Did anyone lie at the trial?"

Bill shrugged his shoulders. "Wasn't it a lie from beginning to end?"

Tring took a cigarette from the packet on the table. He lit it. "Did you ever play the game 'Murder' when you were young? Everybody but the murderer must tell the truth: the murderer may lie."

"How does . . ."

"If you're not the murderer, you've told the truth. But someone else has had to lie to cover himself."

"Hasn't anyone explained to you that this wasn't a game?"

"Listen, Bill, stop being sorry for yourself. You're not the first innocent person who's been found guilty. It's happened before in England and it happens every day of the week in some countries. Start counting your blessings. You're in a country that may still listen seriously to your claim of innocence and you've persuaded me to be mad enough to risk everything for you."

"You're risking something?"

Tring spoke simply, but impressively. "I'm willing to do something that's completely unjustifiable unless the ends can justify the means. If you are proved innocent, any action of mine must be morally right. If you aren't, my action must be wrong no matter how sincere my motives."

Bill shook his head slowly, bewildered to find someone who was willing to risk so much. "I don't think anyone lied."

Tring tried to check both his impatience and his fear.
If there had been no lies, how could there be an effective
appeal: had he already gone too far? "Take it calmly.
Work your mind through the evidence and the people
who gave it. The caretaker gave evidence of the finding
of the body and the girl's father identified it. There
doesn't seem much there . . ."

"George lied."

"When?" snapped Tring.

"When he said Sheila hadn't told him she had a car
to take her home."

Tring began to beat a tattoo on the table with his
fingers.

"He also said he didn't see me and Sheila leaving
the photography room."

"We've been through that. You don't know whether
that's a lie, or not."

"If the other was, this probably is."

Tring's fingers became still. "You're certain George
Willon was told by her that she was getting a lift home?"

"I was there. In any case, at the trial . . ."

"At the trial, Gonchera tackled him on this subject,
but the judge refused any further questions. I wonder
if that's . . ." Tring became silent.

Bill spoke angrily. "You said it would be the murderer who lied. But the police are certain George didn't
kill her."

"Yet if he had been there . . ." Once again, Tring
did not finish the sentence. He pulled his brief-case
nearer to him and opened it, searched amongst the
papers and pulled one out. "Here is a notice of appeal
which has to be signed by you and then sent on by me
to the Registrar of the Court of Criminal Appeal."

Bill borrowed Tring's pen to sign the form. Appeal
was a word of hope. He suffered the bitter, painful
sweetness of restored hope.

: :   : :

Tring drove back to Ashford and Green's house.

Green spoke quickly, the moment he came face to face with Tring. "I'm not going to do it. It's not right and I'm not going to do it."

Tring stepped into the house. This man was not going to mess up the wild gamble that he, Tring, was determined to make.

CHAPTER XIII

XXXXXXXXXXXXXXXXXXXXXXXX XXXXXXXXXXXXXXXXXXXXXXXX

THE APPEAL was held in the Royal Courts of Justice. The three judges were under the presidency of Mr. Justice Onega, a man who had been on the Bench for twenty-two years and looked like it.

Bill was in the dock, guarded by a warder, present as of right since the appeal was not solely on a point of law. A number of reporters were present, as well as a few members of the public. If Bill turned sufficiently to the left, he could see his father, sitting at the end of the third row of benches. His father had aged since the trial: there were lines on his face that Bill had not seen before.

"My Lords," said Gonchera, "I am applying for a writ of *venire facias de novo juratores.*"

"A rather unusual application," observed Mr. Justice Onega, and he appeared to sniff.

"But, I respectfully submit, the right one in the circumstances. It is my contention, as your lordships will realise, that on the evidence I shall be presenting to this court justice can only be done, and be seen to be done, by an order to summon and swear a fresh jury to try the case again from the beginning."

"Is this necessary?" said the youngest of the three

judges. "Could you not have dealt with the matter as an ordinary appeal, either of law only, or a mixture of law and fact?"

"I think not, my Lord."

"I don't know that I agree with you, Mr. Gonchera."

Gonchera was a man well able to conduct his case in the court of appeal—whose atmosphere was very different from the court of first instance and was in many ways almost academic—with a calm judgment even when the presiding judges appeared to show an immediate hostility towards the appellant's case.

"Very well," said the president, when counsel was silent.

"My Lords, I think I should make it clear that the evidence you will hear was brought to the attention of the defence only after the trial of the accused had been completed."

"How did the defence come to learn about it, Mr. Gonchera?" asked the president.

"As to that point, my Lord, perhaps it would be best if your lordships heard about it from the witness's own lips?"

"Why? Are you trying to make a mystery of the facts? Why should we not be told the facts immediately?"

Gonchera leaned back and rested his elbows on the desk behind him. He half turned his head and spoke to Geraldine Pawley in a whisper. "They're a ripe trio of bastards to-day."

She chuckled.

"Well?" said the president sharply, as if his imagination had suggested to him what counsel's words had been.

"On the point that your lordship has just raised, the juror in question sought out the accused's solicitor and told him what had happened."

"Why did he wait until after the trial? Would not a

man of ordinary common sense have realised the necessity for speaking sooner?"

"Perhaps it would be better if your lordships questioned him, rather than me, on that point."

"Very well." Mr. Justice Onega leaned back in his chair.

"My Lords," said Gonchera, "before the trial had begun, one of the jurors, Mr. Green, was walking through the corridors beyond the assize court in order to try to discover where he should report . . ."

"Why weren't strict directions given to him?"

"I've no idea, my Lord."

"Typical," said the judge, with satisfaction.

"Mr. Green was about to ask for directions from two policemen when he realised they were talking to each other. He therefore decided to wait until they had finished. It thus so happened that he overheard part of their conversation. One man said that the trial was liable to be a long one and that he couldn't think why the prisoner did not plead guilty. The second man agreed and then—Mr. Green will testify that he cannot remember the exact words used—said: 'He's been had up for mucking around with women before. Given two years last time to teach him to cool down.'

"Mr. Green was called as a juror in the trial of Regina v. Stemple. He retired with the other eleven men and women at the end of the trial to consider the verdict. He will tell you that he had very great doubts about the guilt of the accused and freely said so, to the extent at one point the jury went back into court to say they could not agree. The judge, very properly, suggested they consider the matter further and they retired again. Once in their room, the other eleven jurors all vehemently attacked Mr. Green for being so stupid and pig-headed. It was at this point of time that Mr. Green remembered the conversation between the two policemen and, by a very natural assumption, thought that he had been hearing about the accused. My Lords, if a man has been convicted once of 'mucking around with women' it is much more likely that a second action against him is correctly based."

"That's a monstrous thing to say," objected the president.

"Has Mr. Green not heard of the maxim, *semper praesumitur pro negante*?" asked the youngest judge.

"Possibly, but I venture to suggest his familiarity with it is unlikely to be when couched in such form. My Lords, we are not concerned here with standards of perfection, but with the standards of everyman. If I know that the man I am trying for theft has a previous conviction for theft, a strong presumption is raised in my mind that he is likely to be guilty of the second offence."

"Are you putting that forward as an eternal proposition?"

"Only, my Lords, as everyman."

"I refuse to believe that everyman can be so naïve."

"Then, my Lord, why is it that the law does not allow a man's previous convictions to be given in open court until the jury has reached and delivered their verdict?"

Gonchera waited for some comment, but there was none. He continued. "My Lords, the fact is that in this case Mr. Green agreed to a verdict of guilty because he believed, quite wrongly, that the conversation he had overheard referred to the accused. His evidence will be that but for this misconception, he would never have agreed to such a verdict.

"My Lords, the right to grant a writ of *Venire de novo* was not affected by the Criminal Appeal Act of 1907. This writ lies where there has been a mistrial because of several alternative causes, one of which is misconduct on the part of the jury discovered after judgment. It is my submission that there has been misconduct here, although such misconduct was entirely fortuitous."

" Mr. Gonchera," said the president, as he opened a text book, " it has been held more than once that where an indictment is good and the jury have been properly empanelled and sworn, and a good verdict is returned, then a *Venire de novo* will not lie although there may well have been conduct on the part of the jury which the court considers unsatisfactory."

" Quite so, my Lord. But in a leading case where, before the summing-up, members of the jury had conversed with witnesses for the prosecution and it was ascertained that such witnesses could in no way be prejudiced by what they had heard, it was held that the prisoner had not been prejudiced even though there had been improper conduct on the part of the jurymen. This, my Lord, underlines my point. The fact to be considered is whether the prisoner has been prejudiced and surely no one can say that my client was not prejudiced? But for what Mr. Green overheard, the verdict would not have been one of guilty: at the very least, there would have been a failure of the jury to reach a verdict."

The president removed the heavy horn-rimmed glasses he wore and rubbed the bridge of his nose. " You are, of course, calling the two policemen, Mr. Gonchera?"

" No, my Lord."

" Why not?"

" Because all efforts have failed to trace them. Or should I say, all efforts have failed to trace two policemen who will admit to having held such a conversation."

" Was there a case in the same Assize Calendar in which a man was accused of some offence against a woman and such man had a previous conviction of the same nature?"

" No, my Lord."

"Your case, Mr. Gonchera, becomes a very insubstantial one."

"My Lord, I submit that we must not concern ourselves with trying to judge Mr. Green's evidence. It surely must be sufficient that he testifies that his decision was affected by what he overheard?"

"But are we then to accept, without question, the word of one man who, had he shown even rudimentary common-sense, should have reported the matter at the beginning of the trial?"

"I would answer that with another question, my Lord. Are we here to judge Mr. Green because he was sufficiently publicly minded to come forward with the truth? Or are we here to see whether Mr. Stemple has suffered an injustice?"

"You are asking that we order a new trial. The cost of such new trial will be considerable, yet to support your application you appear to have only the uncorroborated evidence of one man."

"In the belief that Stemple had a previous conviction of the same nature, Mr. Green was totally unable to perform his duties as a juryman."

"Perhaps, Mr. Gonchera, we should hear your evidence before discussing further the legal problems involved. Suffice it to say for the moment that this court will never be in a hurry to declare a trial void solely on the evidence of a juryman who declares that his verdict was affected by extraneous matters."

: :   : :

The decision of the court was delivered by the president.

"The court allows the appeal and orders that the conviction and judgment be set aside. The appellant will appear at the next Assize and will plead to and answer the indictment which will be in precisely the same form as the abortive indictment on which he has been already tried. The appellant will be retained in custody until the trial."

The judges retired from the courtroom.

Bill's shoulder was tapped. " Let's move, mate." Automatically, he stepped out of the dock into the well of the court. He saw his father, staring at him, and he went to speak, but a hand forced him forward before he knew what to say.

As they walked to the cells, Bill wondered what had been accomplished. What did a new trial mean? Joshua Tring had made it seem as though it must prove his innocence, but surely it could be no more than a repetition of the first one so that in the end he would merely twice suffer public humiliation? George had lied. He would probably successfully lie again. But suppose he did admit he had lied? All the evidence seemed to point to his not being the murderer.

Life imprisonment were two words to scorch and shrivel a man's soul. Better to destroy the life. Then, he imagined what he would be feeling if the sentence had been death and for a second he felt sick.

CHAPTER XIV

xxxxxxxxxxxxxxxxxxxxxxxxxxxxxxxxxxxxxxxxxxx

THE SECOND TRIAL, Regina *v.* Stemple, opened.

Mr. Justice Waring addressed the jury as soon as they were sworn in. " Members of the jury, you cannot be unaware of the fact that the prisoner has been tried in this court before. You will know the result of that trial. Yet you must, for the purpose of this trial, forget your knowledge of the previous trial and judge only on the evidence you hear in this courtroom. Is that perfectly clear?"

Embarrassed by what seemed to be a direct question, two men mumbled " Yes."

When it was certain that the judge was going to say no more, Allenbury stood up. " My Lord, in this case I appear for the Crown." He paused. " The accused is not represented."

The judge folded his long, thin hands together. " Why is that?"

" I cannot answer, my Lord."

The judge turned towards the dock. " Is there a reason for your not being represented, Mr. Stemple?"

Bill, so nervous that his voice became almost squeaky, said: " I want to defend myself, my Lord." That was a hell of a lie for a start, he thought.

" You must be aware that in a very serious case it is essential for a prisoner to be represented?"

Bill made no reply.

" Have you been informed that if you are unable financially to brief counsel, arrangements can be made, nevertheless, for you to be represented?"

" Yes, my Lord."

" Would you like to reconsider your decision? I am prepared to adjourn the court for a short time."

" I want to defend myself."

" Is your solicitor here, Mr. Stemple?" The judge's voice remained level in tone.

Joshua Tring stood up.

" May I have your name, please," said the judge.

" Tring, my Lord."

" Mr. Tring, I desire you to speak to your client and point out, in the strongest possible terms, the reasons why he should have counsel to defend him."

" I have previously tried . . ."

" You will kindly try again."

Tring left the bench in which he had been sitting and, limping slightly, hurried to the dock.

The moment Tring was within earshot, Bill spoke. " For God's sake, let's take his suggestion. I can't . . ."

" You can and will," interrupted Tring. " I told

you, if you defend yourself you'll be allowed to carve a tunnel through the rules of evidence and that's your only hope."

"It sounded reasonable when you suggested it, but . . ."

"And it sounds all right now." Tring turned so that he faced the Bench. His manner was not one that was calculated to soothe Mr. Justice Waring's feelings. "I've spoken to him, my Lord."

"Well?"

"I have tried by every means at my disposal to persuade him, but he remains adamant."

"Have you explained fully the very serious consequences that may reasonably be supposed to attend his action?"

"Indeed, my Lord."

"Then I fear we have no alternative but to proceed." The judge spoke to Allenbury. "Mr. Allenbury, you will kindly remember at all times that the prisoner is not represented."

"Of course, my Lord."

Tring returned to his seat.

"Has the prisoner paper and pencil?" asked the judge.

When Bill said he had not, the clerk of the court began hurriedly to search through the papers in front of him. Allenbury handed a notebook and a pencil to an usher, who carried them to the dock.

Allenbury opened the case for the prosecution.

: :   : :

Mr. Jones gave evidence of identification. At the end of the examination-in-chief, the judge addressed Bill.

"You may cross-examine the witness."

Bill was appalled by the obvious hatred in the quick look the witness gave him.

"Do you wish to question this witness?" asked the judge.

Bill forced his mind to act. " Did you know Sheila was posing for pornographic photos?"

" Of course I didn't."

" Did you know she had four hundred pounds in a banking account?"

" I never asked 'er."

" Didn't she tell you?"

" No, she didn't."

" She never mentioned the money?"

" She weren't in them photos. That wasn't 'er."

" The police proved it was she."

" That don't mean nothing."

" Of course it does."

" Mr. Stemple," said the judge, " the question as to whether this witness does, or does not, believe his daughter was the woman in the photographs is not relevant. As to whether it was she, police evidence will be given later concerning this matter and it will then be up to the jury to accept or reject such evidence."

Bill looked at Tring, who nodded.

There was a short silence. Allenbury stood up. " If there are no more questions?" he asked Bill.

There was a large degree of bitter irony for Bill in the fact that at the first trial, when represented by counsel, he had been almost superfluous to the proceedings and had been consulted about nothing, yet now, when against all logic he was defending himself, he became of some importance. He was actually consulted about his own trial.

Corinne Hammer was called after Patrick Pollard. She gave evidence that she had seen Sheila Jones with George Willon, then with the accused, and that she had seen Sheila Jones leave the annex arm-in-arm with the accused. She had not seen the deceased after that.

Bill cross-examined. " She was an attractive girl, wasn't she?"

Corinne's face became slightly flushed. " I don't know."

" Of course you do."

" I never thought about it."

" You hated her, didn't you?"

" Certainly not."

" You hated her because she was attractive and had fun, which you didn't and couldn't."

" I . . . I wouldn't dream of having that kind of ' fun '."

Allenbury stood up. " It is with some reluctance that I interrupt, my Lord, but I must take objection to the questions."

The judge spoke to Bill. " I will not allow you to put any questions to the witness, Mr. Stemple, that are simply and solely of a scandalous nature."

" But she . . ."

" Please be quiet until I have finished speaking. You have only yourself to blame that you are suffering under a very great handicap in the conduct of your defence. The laws governing the giving and taking of evidence are complex and a matter for expert knowledge. Yet you now have to observe them even though you do not know them and although I shall try to mitigate your difficulties, I can only repeat that the fault is primarily yours.

" You will put questions to the witness which are material ones. Therefore, unless you can persuade me that this witness's private opinion of the deceased girl and her way of life is material, I shall not allow you to put any questions on that subject to her."

" I want to prove she didn't like Sheila."

" Then you will restrict yourself to the possibility of bias. But I warn you that such bias is only relevant if you wish to show that evidence has been given in a biased manner."

Bill stared at Corinne. "You say you saw her with me?"

" Yes."

" Doing what?"

" Dancing."

" And eating and drinking?"

" Yes."

" Having fun, in fact."

" I wouldn't know."

" Were you having fun?"

" Yes."

" How many dances did you have?"

" I don't like dancing."

" How many drinks did you have?"

" I had one."

" Why only one?"

" That was all I wanted."

" And you hate seeing people drink more than one?" She did not answer.

" How do you know Sheila wasn't around after I came up from the basement?"

" I didn't see her."

" Then you were poking and prying everywhere as usual to see what was going on?"

" That's a horrible lie," she said, in a trembling voice.

" Miss Hammer," said the judge, " did you see the deceased after eleven o'clock on that night?"

" No."

" Were you looking for her?"

" Of course not, my Lord."

" Where were you during this time?"

" Either in the conference room or the annex."

" Had she been in either room, would you have seen her?"

" I think so."

The judge put down his pencil. He looked at Bill.

"Are there any more questions you wish to put to this witness?"

Bill looked at Tring and saw the latter shake his head. "No, my Lord."

Allenbury did not re-examine. Janet King was called and after a short examination-in-chief, Bill cross-examined her.

"How was Sheila when she was with me at the head of the stairs?"

"She looked the same as usual," said Janet.

"She wasn't afraid of me?"

"Well, no. I mean, she couldn't have been, considering the way she was behaving."

"Did I look as if I was going to murder her?"

The judge shrugged his shoulders in a weary gesture.

Janet answered the question. "You didn't look as if you were going to do that." Her voice rose at the last word, thereby unintentionally underlining it. There was some laughter.

"When I joined you in the annex, did I look as if I'd just murdered someone?"

"Goodness gracious, no."

"Miss King," said the judge, "when you met the accused and the deceased at the head of the stairs, was either of them carrying anything?"

"She had her handbag."

"Anything else?"

Janet closed her eyes for several seconds, then opened them. "I'm sure there wasn't anything else."

"Neither was in possession of a camera?"

"Oh, no."

"Thank you." The judge wrote in his notebook.

Bill continued. "When I joined you and James, was I terribly upset? Did you think I was in a sweat about something?"

"I . . . I don't think so." She was obviously lying.

Allenbury re-examined. "Can you remember how

L

many drinks the accused had in the ten minutes or quarter of an hour he was with you?"

" A couple, I suppose."

" Thank you."

Carthwright was called.

" Did you think I was terribly upset?" Bill asked, in cross-examination.

" No."

" Did you think I was drinking very heavily?"

" No."

Without the experience to know when to stop, Bill blundered on. " And I wasn't in the least bit nervous?"

Carthwright obviously hesitated. " It just seemed to me you'd had enough to drink," he finally said.

" But you've said I wasn't drinking very heavily."

" Well I . . . Look, it's like this. I thought you'd had a real skinful and that's why you were acting kind of odd. When I said you weren't drinking very heavily I meant that you weren't gulping the stuff down. Not like they are back home when the bar's about to close."

Bill looked at Tring and saw the solicitor was shaking his head. Bill was not surprised. Carthwright had been trying all he knew to help, but because of Bill's stupid ignorance the evidence had ended up by being harmful. Bill began to panic.

Gurren, dressed in his smartest suit, gave his evidence in a smug manner.

" You were too tight to notice anything, weren't you?" demanded Bill loudly.

" Certainly not." Gurren tried to become very dignified.

" You were incapable by midnight."

" I never, never, drink to excess."

" You know you always get tight when the drinks are free."

" Mr. Stemple," said the judge, " how many times do I have to tell you that your cross-examination may not be used to slander witnesses? Mr. Gurren's behaviour on other occasions is of no relevancy to this trial."

"He's lying. How can I prove my innocence if you keep . . ."

"The dangers of the course you have chosen to follow have been more than adequately explained to you." The judge spoke to Allenbury. "Really, Mr. Allenbury, this is a most difficult situation."

"Indeed, my Lord."

The judge questioned the witness. "Mr. Gurren, had you drunk sufficient alcohol to impair your faculties?"

"No, certainly I hadn't. No, definitely not."

"Very well."

Bill's sense of panic increased and became more bitter. Every time he tried to force the truth into the open, the law stepped in and covered it under layers of opaque rules.

"Do you wish to question the witness further?" asked the judge.

"What's the use?" muttered Bill.

The judge questioned Gurren. "Are you saying that had Miss Jones come up from the basement within a short time after the prisoner you would inevitably have seen her, no matter which route she took?"

"Oh, no, my Lord. But I'm certain she never came into the annex."

"Very well."

George Willon entered the courtroom. He took the oath and as he waited for the first question, he brushed the back of his hand across his forehead in a gesture that was strangely sad.

Allenbury's examination-in-chief was almost word for word what it had been at the first trial.

Bill, about to open his cross-examination, noticed his throat had suddenly gone dry. He found difficulty in swallowing. He looked at George, who refused to meet his eyes. What had it been like for George, Bill suddenly thought, living with the knowledge that the girl he had wanted to marry had been murdered?

" Yes, Mr. Stemple?" said the judge sharply.

" You asked her whether you could take her home, didn't you?" demanded Bill to George. " You came up when I was with her and asked her for a dance. You told her that Reg had promised to drive the two of you back. She said she had her own transport."

" No."

" Why are you lying?"

" I'm not."

" You know you're lying. What are you trying to hide? Did you kill her?"

" Kill her? How can *you* say that? I couldn't have hurt a hair on her head and you know it. You know it, you swine," he shouted.

" Why d'you keep lying?"

" I tell you, I'm not."

" You are."

The judge intervened in a quiet, unemotional voice. " Must I explain yet again, Mr. Stemple, that when a witness denies something you must accept that denial unless you can prove the contrary."

Bill spoke wildly. " He's lying. He's doing everything he can to see me guilty."

" You will control yourself."

" Control myself? When I know he's lying?" Bill shouted at George. " You're lying to try to get your own back on me."

" Stop this," ordered the judge.

Bill ignored the command. " You were so jealous of me, you'd do anything."

George shouted back. " You ruined her."

" If necessary, I will adjourn the court," said the judge.

" Ruin her?" repeated Bill, with furious sarcasm. " She didn't take much persuading to come out with me."

"Oh, God! You ruined her. You made her pose for those terrible photographs."

"I wasn't taking them."

The courtroom filled with the sounds of voices of people who no longer whispered to each other but spoke aloud. The usher vainly called for silence.

Through the noise, Bill heard his name being called. He looked down and was surprised to see Tring.

"Use your bloody brains," said Tring. "Get on to the corridor."

Automatically, and without thought, Bill put the questions that Tring had told him to put. "Why d'you think it was I who took those photos?"

"I knew it." George was suffering from an excess of grief and anger which left him not fully aware of what he was saying.

"Why? Because you saw the two of us leave the photography room at midnight?"

"I didn't think it was anyone in the firm. I knew what was going on and when I saw you both come out of there I suddenly knew it was you. If I'd had the guts to kill you, I would have done. I'd have killed you, d'you hear? Christ, I'd have killed you."

Allenbury was on his feet trying to address the judge, as was the clerk of the court: both ushers were calling for silence: the public, the Press, and the jury, were talking.

"Be quiet," said the judge loudly. The authority in his voice was so great that within seconds the noise died away. "Has the shorthand writer been able to record the witness's answers?"

The clerk of the court questioned the shorthand writer, who sat on his left. He stood up, turned right round, and spoke to the judge.

"It appears," said the judge, "that the shorthand writer has been able to record most of what has been said. Because of the very great importance of this evidence, I intend to adjourn the court for a quarter of an hour. Mr. Tring will consult the accused and will discover whether, in the circumstances, he wishes to change his mind and be respresented by counsel."

In the witness-box, George seemed to be about to cry.

CHAPTER XV

JOSHUA TRING, in London, entered the new building in Temple Court and walked up the stairs to the first floor. He knocked on the inner door, the outer one was swung back to show the list of the members of chambers, and went inside. The clerks' room was on the right and Justin was just coming out of it.

" I've got to have a word with Mr. Gonchera," said Tring, in a manner even more abrupt than usual.

"Dear me, Mr. Tring, we weren't expecting . . ."

" I know, I know. I've no appointment and that's enough to make the heavens collapse."

Justin, he had been chief clerk for so long there was a dusty patina about him, looked very upset. The junior clerk, sitting at the smaller of the desks, grinned.

" Mr. Gonchera's wanted for the Stemple case, bloody smartly," said Tring.

" I beg your pardon, Mr. Tring?"

" Call him out."

" I fail to understand this. We were under the impression, the somewhat unfortunate impression, that you did not desire to brief us again."

" All right, all right, things became a trifle un-orthodox. But I haven't been struck off the Rolls yet, so let's get down to business."

" I regret," said Justin, with what could have been

satisfaction, " that we have gone special up north. A very fine brief : very fine indeed."

" Are you telling me he isn't available?"

" We are certainly not available, Mr. Tring, for a case in which we had been given the impression that we were not to be briefed, despite the fact . . ."

Tring said three words which brought Justin's booming voice to an abrupt halt. " What about Miss Pawley?" continued Tring. " Are you going to grin all over your face and say she's gone special in the Scilly Islands?"

" No, Mr. Tring."

" I'll give her the brief, then, rather than bring in a new silk who hasn't been with the case."

" Miss Pawley has a very great deal of work in hand."

" A hundred guineas on the brief and twenty-five for the conference."

" Very busy, Mr. Tring. The work has been . . ."

" Call it a hundred and fifty and stop haggling. And I want the conference now."

" Very well, Mr. Tring. Perhaps if it's urgent we should try to overlook the unconventional manner in which things have been handled." Justin spoke to his junior clerk. " Kindly make some coffee for Mr. Tring, who does not drink tea."

" You've a memory like an elephant's," said Tring, as he sat down in a very worn wing-back chair. " And what's more, you're a bloody rascal over fees."

Justin left the room, but not before a stirring of his facial muscles suggested he was not displeased by what had been said.

: :   : :

By nine o'clock the next morning, there was a long queue outside the entrance into the public gallery and, despite repeated warnings from attendant policemen that only the first hundred people would gain admittance, the queue continued to grow.

Henry Stemple waited in the main hall. Neither he nor Margaret had slept the previous night for more than a few moments at a time. Questions had raced through their minds and smashed into one another to explode into a welter of hope and fear.

In his cell below the courts, Bill waited, prey to emotions more mixed than any he had known before. George *had* been in the basement. What did that mean within the context of the murder? Would the evidence clear him, Bill? Would it inculpate George? But hadn't all the police evidence proved that George could not possibly be the murderer?

In the ladies' robing room, Geraldine Pawley sat at the table on which rested her red bag, wig box, gown, and several text books. She was red-eyed from working through most of the night and stabs of tiredness swirled through her brain.

Driving in his Sunbeam Rapier, at too high a speed, Tring sang in a reasonably musical bass voice. He had risked everything in an effort to help a man who had been beaten by authority and the masses. And the risk had been justified. No one knew what was going to happen now, but he maintained a simple faith in the simple belief that his cause was righteous and therefore must flourish.

In a large Victorian house, known as the draughtiest judges' lodgings in all seven circuits, Mr. Justice Waring watched his Marshal eat the last piece of toast in the rack. The Marshal was not the kind of man Waring would have chosen to eat with. An honourable Marshal left the last piece of toast for the judge. He thought about the case. He was certain that the defence had engineered all that had happened: the solicitor was a man with few professional scruples when it came to gaining what he considered to be justice. Should the jury find Stemple innocent then in his, Waring's, opinion any means used to bring about that decision were justified. He had an almost fanatical regard for the law of England, but this regard was not so great, as with some of his fellow judges, that the need to uphold it was greater than the need to do justice.

He watched the Marshal pour himself another cup of tea. Did the wretched man never stop eating and drinking?

George Willon, having arrived an hour too early, spent most of that hour wishing he had had the courage to commit suicide during the night.

: :   : :

" My Lord," said Geraldine Pawley, " I have a request to make on behalf of the defence. Due to events yesterday, it became clear that the accused's interests would best be served were he represented by counsel. I therefore now have to request the court that I be allowed to appear for the accused." Her voice had the rare, for a female, quality that it carried easily without being too highly pitched.

The judge nodded. " In my opinion, Miss Pawley, that is the only possible course of conduct and I feel certain Mr. Allenbury will raise no objection."

Allenbury stood up. He rubbed his square jaw with his right hand, then dropped his hand. " In a great many ways, my Lord, I welcome the arrangement."

" Very well."

George Willon went into the box.

Geraldine Pawley adjusted her wig with a deft movement of her two hands that was entirely feminine. " You gave certain evidence yesterday, Mr. Willon, which obviously has very great bearing on the case. I should like to take you slowly over that evidence once more."

George's face was white. His hands were shaking and he kept them by his side to try to hide them.

" Mr. Willon, were you aware before the night of

Friday the twelfth of June, that Sheila Jones was posing for pornographic photographs?"

He twice tried to answer, but each time could not speak the words. He swallowed heavily.

" Were you, Mr. Willon?"

" Yes," he muttered.

" How did you find out?"

" We were out one day on a picnic. She . . . she asked me to get something out of her handbag for her. I came across an envelope with fifty pounds in it."

" What did you do?"

" Does it . . . matter?"

" It matters a very great deal."

" I asked her jokingly whether she'd been robbing a train."

" And she answered?"

" She made some comment and I wouldn't believe her. I . . . I got all jealous. We had a row over the money and in the end she got so angry she told me the truth. The moment she'd told me, she was horrified by what she'd done. She made me swear never to repeat it."

" How did the news affect you?"

" I felt sick. I couldn't believe she'd do such a thing. She'd always been so . . . so nice."

" Did this alter your friendship with her?"

" I can't . . . I couldn't . . . ." George unaware of what he was doing, reached up to his collar and ran his forefinger round the inside of it as if it were choking him. Then he gripped the edge of the witness-box with both hands. He spoke as quickly as he could. " She told me she was making a lot of money. She'd always wanted money because somehow she thought it was all that mattered. She told me she'd have married me if I'd more money. She said she was going to make enough to be able to buy the kind of house she wanted, in a neighbourhood where people didn't walk around in their braces. She told me that if I couldn't do that for her, she'd have to do it for herself."

" What did you think that meant?"

" That she'd marry me when she had enough money. That's what was so terrible. You've got to understand. Oh, God, it hurt! I loved her and it revolted me to know how she was making money, but . . ." He stared with pathetic appeal at Geraldine Pawley. " Can't you see? If she didn't make it, she'd never have the house she had to have before she married me."

" You knew that if you were ever to marry her, she had to pose for the photographs?"

George leaned against his hands which were still clutching the front of the box. " I know what it sounds like. Every time I went into the house, I'd be reminded of how it had been bought. But I loved her . . ."

" What really happened on the night she was killed?"

George looked round the courtroom. " She danced with me, then she went with him. She'd always liked being with him because of his position and money, but I knew he'd never marry her. I asked her for another dance, but she refused. Then I told her I'd fixed up with Reg for a lift home, but she said she'd already arranged everything. After she'd gone off with him, I drank and danced with one or two of the others. I'd had too much drink and suddenly decided that if I'd any guts I'd go and find her and take her away from him. I searched upstairs and she wasn't there. I went to the basement."

There was a complete silence. Geraldine Pawley broke it. " And then?"

George started, almost as if he had forgotten where he was. He licked his lips. " I stepped out of the boiler room into the passage and saw them coming out of the photography room. I ducked out of sight, even though it had been them I wanted to see. I suddenly wondered why they'd been in the photography room and then I remembered the photos. The thought made me sick. I left the basement the back way and went to the dance room. All the time, I kept imagining him taking those photos. When I got home, my mind wouldn't leave me alone."

" What happened when you were told about the death of Sheila Jones and the circumstances surrounding it?"

" I knew she'd been posing for him and I prayed every night he'd be caught."

" Is that why you denied Sheila had told you she had her own transport home?"

Allenbury did not object to the question.

" If people thought he'd lied once, they'd think he'd lied time and time again," said George.

" Is that why you have never admitted until to-day that you saw them both leaving the photography room, as Mr. Stemple has always claimed it was probable you did?"

" I wasn't going to help him."

" But if when the accused left the photography room Sheila Jones was alive did it not occur to you that perhaps he had had nothing to do with the killing?"

" He must have gone back later. He took the photos and then killed her."

" Your motives weren't entirely based on revenge, were they? After all, if you'd given honest evidence, the police would soon have realised that you knew all along that the photos were being taken?"

He stared at her, unable to hide his dreadful misery.

: :   : :

Allenbury was re-examining.

" You have testified that you saw them when they left the photography room. We know that that time was approximately midnight. Have you any idea when it was you returned to the dance floor?"

" It was straight away."

" Where did you go?"

" To the conference room."

" Did you speak to anyone?"

" Yes."

" How long were you there?"

" Until the dance ended."

" And then what happened?"

" I went home with Reg."

" Can you tell the court what the time was when you and he parted?"

" I just don't know. We finished some beer he had in his car and then I went inside my house and he drove away."

" Did you speak to anyone in your house?"

" I woke my father up. There was a row because I was so tight. He had to help me up to my bed. And then I kept imagining them as he took the photos. . . ."

                    : :   : :

Geraldine Pawley's closing speech was pitched on a low and even note.

". . . You have heard, members of the jury, that at about midnight Sheila Jones and William Stemple left the photography room and went up the stairs. The accused left her, alive, as she returned down the stairs and he went into the annex. When the dance ended, he joined Mr. Breslow. From Mr. Breslow's car he went to his own and as you have heard from Miss King, he called out good night to her and Mr. Carthwright. He drove back to Ashford and by the grace of God, in such mysterious ways does God work, he was stopped by a policeman and taken to Ashford police station as being drunk in charge of a car. He was not released until one-thirty-three in the morning.

" Now if we examine these times in conjunction with other evidence we find that from midnight, when we

now know that Miss Jones was alive, until one-thirty-
three the defendant could not have gone down to the
photography room to take photographs or to kill her.
To drive from Ashford to Leamarsh would have taken
him at least twenty minutes. The earliest, therefore,
at which he could have arrived back at Leamarsh was
one-fifty-three. Members of the jury, the police evidence
is that the deceased met her death between eleven-thirty
and one-thirty and one-thirty is twenty-three minutes
before William Stemple could possibly have returned to
Leamarsh."

: :   : :

Allenbury was even more painstakingly thorough than
ever.

" . . . The defence, members of the jury, has over-
looked this. If William Stemple is not the murderer, who
is? We know that George Willon is innocent and not
a breath of suspicion has rested on any other person
from the beginning to the end of this trial.

" Naturally, counsel for the defence has made great
play with the fact that the earliest time at which the
prisoner could have returned to Leamarsh was twenty-
three minutes after the latest time at which the medical
evidence places the time of death. But the medical
experts themselves said that the times were not scientific
facts and could be no more than guides. There is
nothing wrong in changing those times if facts suggest,
as strongly as do the facts in this case, that they must
logically be changed. What is a mere twenty-three
minutes? No, members of the jury, the knowledge that
the prisoner did not return to Leamarsh until about
one-fifty-three—it could have been earlier had he driven
recklessly—does not preclude your finding him guilty
of this sordid murder.

" Let us consider the other evidence. There are two
hundred pounds in one-pound notes which the prisoner

paid into his bank and which he claims he won at Folkestone races, a claim in support of which he cannot bring one tittle of evidence. There is his finger-prints on the murder weapon. There are the two letters written to the dead man, Mr. Heavers, typed on the type-writer in his room. There are . . ."

:: ::

The foreman of the jury delivered the verdict. "Not guilty."

CHAPTER XVI

xᴏᴏᴏᴏᴏᴏᴏᴏᴏᴏᴏᴏᴏᴏᴏᴏᴏᴏᴏᴏᴏᴏᴏᴏᴏᴏᴏᴏᴏᴏᴏᴏᴏᴏᴏx

WHEN BILL WALKED into the kitchen of Straightacres Farm, immediately ahead of his father, his mother looked at him with wild disbelief. After a while, she said: "Bill . . . Bill . . ."

"Not guilty," said Henry Stemple.

"Oh, my God!" she murmured.

They became embarrassed by their openly displayed emotions and tried to act more calmly.

"I bought a bottle of Heidsieck," said Henry Stemple.

"Then get the glasses," she said softly, "and stop talking."

He smiled at her, with infinite understanding, then went through to the sitting-room. "Who did it, Bill?" she asked, so quietly she was almost whispering.

Bill sat down. "I don't know. They say it can't have been George. I just don't know." He felt drained of mental and physical strength.

Henry Stemple returned with three deep, thin, cham-pagne glasses. "It won't be as chilled as it ought to be . . ."

"Does it matter?" she asked. "This isn't a drink, Henry, it's a medicine."

"To hell with that! I could have bought a bottle of cough syrup at a twentieth of the price."

"You know perfectly well what I mean, you old fool."

He untwisted the wire cage over the cork, which immediately blew out. Champagne began to gush over the floor. There was much shouting and laughter before Bill held a glass under the bottle.

The toast was a simple one.

Bill drained his glass. He lit a cigarette. "D'you know the funniest thing of all?"

"What?"

"They'll probably have to take me back at Lanfairs. The maharaja may well catch a thrombosis thinking about it."

An hour and a half later, Bill said good night and went slowly up the twisting staircase to his bedroom. He opened the door and stepped in. He was back with the fourteen-inch wide floorboards, the wall and ceiling beams, the old oak dressing-table, the Persian rug, the bed, and the cupboard built in to the space behind the huge central chimney. With the exception of the bed, all these things were old. He had thought he would never see them again, but now he was returned to them. He crossed to the window and looked out. It was just on sunset. The land swept down and away, a patterned criss-cross of browns and greens: in the distance, sharp in outline because there had recently been rain, was the horizon.

He drew the curtains. It was years since he had gone to bed so early, but he was tired to the point where it was a painful effort to keep his eye-lids open. He undressed. The cell bed had squeaked at every movement and the blankets had smelled of age. His bed was silent and the linen smelled of the lavender bundles his mother used.

It was very strange to have a window unprotected by bars. But for Joshua Tring, he would still be facing bars. Joshua Tring was an anachronism: he still believed in certain things.

: :   : :

At 7.30 a.m. Shute climbed out of bed and stood on the carpet.

"You're getting fatter," said his wife, as she zipped up her skirt. She became almost sylph-like when compared to him.

"Nonsense," he retorted.

"It's the diet sheet again for you, Alec."

He muttered something that he was careful she should not hear. If a man was fat by nature, he was happier and better off fat . . .

"Alec, did he do it?"

He stripped off the brightly coloured pyjama jacket. "Having heard that new evidence at the trial, no, I don't think he did."

"Just from reading the reports it seemed as if he might still have done it, in spite of the evidence of that little pimp."

"If you women concerned yourselves with your own business, you wouldn't all talk so damn' daft." He put on his shirt. "George Willon was and is a desperately unhappy person."

"He was willing to live off her."

"He loved her to the point where he'd suffer anything rather than lose her."

"That, Alec, is a really classical excuse for a pimp. I suppose they come to you, with the tears in their eyes, begging you not to arrest them because they love all their lady friends so?"

He chuckled.

M

"One egg and one rasher of bacon," she said.

"Now look here, in my office is a mountain of work. . . ."

"And only one piece of toast." She left the room.

He finished dressing. Perhaps he should not have laughed at her. Still, on past experience, the diet would only last a couple of days, just until his openly expressed misery had an effect.

Later, he drove the mile and a quarter to the police station. Once in his office, he checked the mail, throwing as much of it into the waste-paper basket as he dared.

Marrins knocked and entered. "'Morning, sir. A breaking and entering has just come through from Coldborrow."

Shute looked up. "Is it a big one?"

"I spoke to the wife over the telephone and she said the house was stripped of a fortune. Then the husband took over and said there wasn't very much missing."

"Nip along in a minute and get them to sing the same story." Shute turned and looked out of the window. "How d'you place William Stemple?"

Marrins sat down : "A right lucky bastard."

"You're saying there's no doubt he did it?"

"I'll lay five to one with anyone."

"Why did he drive off home, then? Wouldn't he have waited around until it was O.K. to take the photos?"

"He wanted to make certain no one would so much as suspect what he was up to. It wasn't any good hanging round, for fear of late departing amorous couples. So he cleared right off and drove back to Ashford, as if going home. If the police hadn't picked him up, he'd have returned to Lanfairs."

"Then what did actually happen?"

"When he was released by the police, he went back. The girl had had to wait for him because she had no car. They began photographing. His blood got overheated because of what was going on. He hit her with the tripod, meaning to daze her sufficiently to let him get on with it, but she had this thin skull. He'd killed her and that was enough to stop all his ideas dead in their tracks. If the medical evidence had stretched the possible time of death up to two o'clock he'd have been a sitting duck at the trial. The jury were senile. Just because the prosecution's case fell down on one small point, they went stupid. So she was alive when they left the photography room. Didn't the jury hear that the times of death were elastic? He killed her whenever it was he got back to Lanfairs."

" It wasn't that simple for the jury."

" It should have been."

" Haven't you ever been interested by the psychology of juries? The prosecution gave times, and then said they were elastic, but the jury wouldn't acknowledge them as elastic once they had been specifically given. Those were the times and when it seemed they were wrong, the jury saw the evidence itself as being wrong. To a jury, the prosecution's evidence must be like Cæsar's wife. The moment it isn't, they illogically reach over on the side of the prisoner. In this case, they saw with the new piece of evidence Willon supplied them with and their own newly acquired bias that the prisoner *could* have been innocent. That was enough for them. And, I'll say it, rightly so."

" You won't get me agreeing."

" No, I suppose not. You haven't thought about the girl, have you?"

" What about her?"

" She was a prude."

" Then I'll start collecting photos of broad-minded girls."

" Try supposing she really was prudish."

" That's a strain that could injure."

Shute might not have heard. " A prude who suffered

more than most from the modern disease, ' I want.'
Suffered from it so badly that she's tempted into posing.
How would she reconcile her need for the money with
her modesty?"

" What did you call it?"

" Wipe your mind with a sponge."

" Yes, sir," said Marrins shortly.

" We saw her photographs. In each one of them, her
head was turned away so that you never saw her face."

" Yes, sir."

" Got any fags?"

Marrins wondered whether to say he had none, but
deemed it more prudent to produce a packet.

Shute lit his cigarette. He dropped the used match
into an ash-tray. " Last night, I was thinking. Was
it Stemple, wasn't it Stemple? That didn't take me
anywhere, so I said it wasn't Stemple. Who then?
It wasn't Willon.

" I separated the evidence. Stemple took the girl into
the photography room and the tripod was on the couch
as he said it was. He picked it up and put it on the
floor. He tried to mess around with her, but she wasn't
having any because he refused to speak the magic
word ' marriage.' They left. The girl reached the stairs
and then said she'd forgotten her handbag. She told
him not to wait and he was so fed up that he reckoned
he damned well wouldn't wait.

" Now for the other part of the evidence. She went
back to the photography room. Eventually, the photographer turned up and gave her fifty quid for the last
effort. They got cracking on taking the new set of
photos. Several shots were taken, perhaps all that
were going to be, and then an argument started. An
argument not about sex, as we've always claimed, but
about money. She wanted a bigger share. The photographer, in a wild rage, picked up the first thing to
hand and lashed out. It wasn't a heavy blow, for one

reason or another, and normally it wouldn't have killed. But the girl had a thin skull."

" Why should an argument about money have led to that great a rage, sir?"

" It's obvious. Just as it's now obvious why the blow wasn't a harder one. And there were no finger-prints because the photographer was wearing gloves. Are you with me?"

" Only in the flesh, sir, not the spirit."

" D'you remember the two letters to Heavers?"

" Of course."

" They were written on Stemple's typewriter. Assume he's innocent and this suggests a deliberate attempt to frame him if ever there was trouble: but when they were written, there couldn't have been any suggestion there ever would be trouble. If it wasn't to frame him, then what?" Shute leaned forward. " Perhaps a sub-conscious gesture of hate and humiliation? A secret desire to use something of his in the disgusting business?"

Marrins spoke almost scornfully. " Isn't that getting a bit daft?"

" Is it?"

" Secret desires of humiliation have always seemed daft to me, sir."

Shute heaved himself to his feet. " You've always had your two feet very solidly on the ground. But human nature isn't always solid. An abnormal mind can do and think anything, as you ought to know. It's a stupid policeman who's surprised by something some-one's done."

Marrins did not say that his definition of a stupid policeman differed somewhat from that.

" Have a think about the incredible manœuvres the killer took to preserve his secret," said Shute. " But why bother? Why muck around with all that business of leaving the money in a tree in Hyde Park? If Heavers had discovered the identity of the sender of the photos, he'd never have disclosed it because he'd have had far too much to lose. And we've checked that none of the staff of Lanfairs could have been known to Heavers. So it was an incredible precaution taken when no precaution was necessary. What does that tell you?"

"I . . . I beg your pardon, sir?"

"You haven't listened to a bloody word I've said."

"Of course I have, sir. It was just . . ."

"Skip it." Shute kicked the waste-paper basket out of his way and sat down on his chair, to the usual accompaniment of wooden creaks. "The killer watched an innocent Stemple tried and convicted of murder and sentenced to life imprisonment. You've got to hate someone pretty hard before you can do that. The human conscience is a ruddy powerful weapon."

"Yes, sir."

"The killer hated Stemple."

"Yes, sir."

Shute looked at Marrins. "Sometimes, I don't think . . . never mind. Just go with me on one thing," he continued. "Is there any aspect of this case we never bothered to investigate fully?"

Marrins thought. "No, sir."

"Well, there was. We didn't check on how the killer knew to write Heavers in the first place, asking him if he wanted photographs. So go and search through Heavers's books, do it personally and don't leave it to the London boys, and note down every name and address in Kent to which he sent his photos."

"The whole county, sir?"

"That's right."

Marrins sighed.

: :   : :

When Bill entered Parry's office that morning he was not surprised to see how embarrassed Parry was. "The return of the prodigal son," he said.

" Yes, I suppose . . ." Parry did not finish the sentence. " Glad to see you back, Bill."

There was a silence.

" How's the Eight Fifty going?" asked Bill.

" Not too badly, not too badly. One or two faults have cropped up, of course, but they're talking about putting them right for next year. We're looking for a new slogan for the second-wave publicity in the nationals."

" Hasn't Tired Tim come up with something?"

" He did suggest: ' Never have so many motorists driven so far for so little.' We felt that wasn't really original enough."

There was another silence.

" I'm really glad to have you back, Bill. Really glad. Carthwright is moving out of your room. It's really rather fortunate that we couldn't find a suitable replacement for you."

" Very fortunate," agreed Bill dryly.

Soon afterwards, he left and crossed the passage to his room.

Carthwright, sitting behind the desk, looked up. " Killed any good blondes lately?"

Bill stifled the anger he felt. He looked round. " I expected to find Janet in here."

" Just gone out for a breather. She gets exhausted rather quickly these days."

" Should I congratulate you both on a forthcoming happy event?" Bill was more than satisfied by the look on the other's face.

: :   : :

Detective Constable Marrins caught the four o'clock from Charing Cross to Ashford and then drove north up the A20 to Leamarsh. He reported to Shute.

" Here's the list, sir." He handed several sheets of paper to the D.I. " Three hundred and fifty names. Only Middlesex was more popular."

"I always said the men of Kent had dirty minds."
Shute began to read through the list of names, marking
some of them with a pencil. When he reached the end,
he looked up. "They could work for Lanfairs, we just
don't know, never having checked through all the workers. So we'll begin with a geographical circle taking in
Maidstone and Ashford."

: :   : :

Bridges looked frightened. "Photographs?" he croaked.

The uniformed constable nodded. "That's right. Red-
hot, so they say. Your name was on the mailing list."

"I don't know anything . . ."

"We're not gunning for you because of that. D'you
work at Lanfairs?"

"Me? I'm a jobbing gardener. And look, I didn't
get them photos because of what you're thinking."

"Look, mate, I'm broad-minded. Every man to his
pastime. D'you know anyone who works at Lanfairs?"

"Me brother-in-law."

"Who's he?"

"Bert Breslow."

"Did he know anything about the photos?"

"I used to pass some of 'em on to Bert."

The constable began to write in his notebook.

"'Ere, you said you wasn't doing nothing about it."

"Don't fret, chum. Your secret's safe with the silent
force."

: :   : :

Albert Breslow was digging in the allotment he hired
from the council when Detective Inspector Shute spoke
to him.

"You again," muttered Bert. "I thought the bloody
thing was over and done with."

"You've got a brother-in-law called Bridges."

"It's a misfortune, but it ain't a crime."

"Did he used to give you photographs?"

Bert suddenly became deeply interested in his digging. " Who did you show them to?"

" The boys, like."

" Who does that mean?"

" The boys in Dispatch and Printing. Good for a giggle, some of 'em."

" Did anyone from P.R.O. or Advertising see them?"

Bert dug the heavily-tined fork into the thick clay soil. He scraped his right boot on the crossbar.

" Let's have the history," snapped Shute.

" Me and the boys were looking when she walks in, as bitchy as ever. I tried to shove 'em back in me pocket and missed and they fell on the floor. She was near enough to see what they was. I thought she was going to faint, like. Then, not saying nothing, she bent down and picked 'em up and holding 'em like they was stinking, she left."

" Was Heavers's address on any of them?"

" There was a name and address. Like as if I might want to send for some. Which I didn't."

" Thanks," said Shute.

CHAPTER XVII

×××

BILL WAS LOOKING through the file of Italian newspaper cuttings, resulting from the visit of the Italian journalists, when the inter-com buzzed. It was Mrs. Berry from reception.

" Two detectives would like to speak to you, Mr. Stemple."

What did they want now? Hadn't they shattered enough of his life? " Send 'em up," he said harshly.

He stood up. He remembered that Joshua Tring and his wife were coming to dinner that evening. He, Bill, had never been prepared to look up to anyone, but now he looked up to Tring.

He walked across to the door, opened it, and stepped out into the corridor. There was a rattling from the lift shaft and then the lift arrived. Detective Inspector Shute and Detective Constable Marrins stepped out of it.

Janet King came along the corridor in a dress so tight about her hips that it looked as if it must split at the next waggle. When she saw the detectives, she stopped.

" 'Morning, Miss King," said Shute.

She smiled. " How absolutely thrilling seeing you again. Does that mean there's been another?"

For once, Shute found himself silenced and it was almost with admiration that he watched her leave. He went forward and shook hands with Bill. " Nice of you to spare the time to see us, Mr. Stemple."

" Did I have an option?" demanded Bill, as he turned back into his room. He felt very afraid, yet knew not why.

After they were sitting down, Marrins took a packet of Oliviers from his pocket and offered them.

" I've come for a spot of help, Mr. Stemple," said Shute.

Bill stared at the large detective with a round, pleasant-looking face in which were the two eyes that pierced a man's mind. " Help in what?"

" Tracing out the murderer."

" Why the hell should I do a thing? That's your pigeon and I hope you fry it."

" I can understand how you feel . . ."

" You understand nothing. When were you tried for murder? When did you sit in a cell, knowing that for the rest of your life you were going to do just that? When did you have the world looking at you, trying to work out whether you really did kill someone?"

"That's why I've come to you. When we nail the murderer, people will stop looking at you."

"Are you intending to judge everyone in turn until you get the verdict you want?"

"I'm hoping for a confession."

"From whom?"

"Will you help us?"

"No."

"I'm sorry you're taking this attitude, Mr. Stemple."

"I'll bet you're weeping."

"I'd have thought you'd want to uncover the truth?"

"I want to bury everything."

Shute turned and spoke to Marrins. "Let's have them."

Marrins opened the plastic brief-case he was carrying and took out a photograph album and a quarto sheet of paper. He handed the paper to the D.I.

Shute spoke to Bill. "One of the things that always puzzled me was the source of the two hundred pounds. It didn't come from Folkestone races, certainly. If it didn't come from the obscene photos, why were you hiding its source? I discovered the answers two days ago. They tell me all hell was let loose in these offices when the photograph of the . . ." He looked down at the paper in his hand, "of the Lanfair Eight Fifty appeared in the French Press."

Bill picked up a pencil and fiddled with it. He'd thought he'd cleared himself of all the trouble: now, he found some of it weighing down on him as heavily as ever. To be sacked from Lanfairs after all he had gone through . . .

Shute spoke. "Of course, Lanfairs didn't ask the police to carry out the investigation and in any case,

I'm not certain how much of a police matter it would be."

"Then why bring the subject up?" asked Bill hoarsely. "I thought a little mutual help . . ."

"Why not call it unilateral blackmail?"

Bill dropped the pencil, stubbed out his cigarette.

"I want you to show something to Miss Hammer," said Shute.

"Such as what?"

Shute raised himself sufficiently out of the chair to take the photograph album from Marrins and hand it to Bill.

Bill put the album down and opened it at the first page. "God Almighty!"

"It was Heavers's reference album."

Bill stared wildly at the D.I. "You can't show this to her. She'll take one look and . . . Well anything could happen."

"Corinne Hammer killed the girl, Mr. Stemple."

"She what?"

"She took the photographs and hit the girl with the tripod. That's fact. But as things stand at the moment, we can't prove enough for a court of law. I must have a confession. The only thing that may break open the secret half of her mind is the shock that these photos will give her." Shute leaned back in his chair. His voice became bitter. "Sometimes, we policemen deal with crimes where we're not horrified by the crime or the criminal, but by the tragedy of the criminal's life. Corinne Hammer leads a tragic, bitterly painful life because her thoughts, desires, and actions are ruled by things that disgust her but which she can't ignore, no matter how much she struggles to ignore them. Nature presented her with the kind of face and body that sends a man's desires into cold storage. She couldn't get married to a one-legged dwarf. Because she's only too aware of this, she's forced herself to believe that

relationships between men and women are nauseating—
yet the image of such relationships haunts her subcon-
scious mind.

"She walked into Dispatch when Breslow was looking at some of Heavers's photographs. Breslow dropped
them in the panic and she saw them. She had to pick
them up and take them away, even though she utterly
despised herself for doing so. In her mind, the terrible
hate/attraction conflict became a conflagration."

"How can you be so certain?"

"Sheila Jones was a prude, wasn't she?"

"But the photos . . ."

"Like the rest of the young of to-day, she thought
money meant everything. When she was offered fifty
pounds for every photo accepted she probably refused
to have anything to do with the idea—until it was
pointed out that her face would never show and the
photographer would be a woman. That's how a prude
reconciled her prudity with these photos."

Bill closed up the album.

"Shall we get it over and done with?" asked Shute,
sadly.

Bill stood up.

"Bring the album," said Shute.

::   ::

Corinne Hammer worked in a long, narrow room. On
her desk, no matter at what time of the year, there was
always a glass vase filled with flowers.

She was typing when Bill knocked on the door and
went in, leaving the door half open.

"What do you want, Mr. Stemple?" she asked, her
voice harsh.

"I've brought you something to look at."

"I don't want anything of yours."

He stopped by her desk.

"Go away," she said shrilly. "You're not to come
in here."

He put down the album and opened it.

She stared at the photographs. Her heavy, ugly face became shocked and her mouth opened slightly. After a while, she began to cry.

Shute and Marrins entered the room. Marrins quietly closed the door.

"Did Sheila demand too much money?" asked Shute.

The tears streamed down her face.

"You didn't really mean to kill her, did you?"

She looked up at Shute. "She . . . she said she'd tell everyone. If I didn't pay her a hundred instead of fifty pounds, she'd tell everyone I was taking and selling obscene photos. She said what would Mr. Parry think? She said Mr. Stemple would laugh himself silly. I couldn't let her do that. I didn't know what I was doing, but I just had to stop her leaving. I suddenly found I'd killed her."

"Did it never occur to you that she wouldn't have told anyone because she was far too mixed up in the thing herself?"

Corinne Hammer shook her head.

"How did it start?" asked Shute.

She shuddered. "I saw those photos that Breslow dropped. They made me feel sick. To think that men were so beastly they liked that sort of thing. I brought them up here and went to tear them up. I . . . I looked through them again and then I couldn't tear them up. I tell you, I couldn't. I put them in my drawer and . . . and kept looking at them. I thought about all the men paying money for such filthy things and every time I read the address that was on one of them, I wondered. I hated myself, but I couldn't stop wondering. I thought of making money out of these men . . . I didn't want to write. I swear I didn't."

"Did Sheila Jones take much persuading?"

"I knew how desperately she liked money. So I told

her she could make a lot out of posing in the nude. She called me a dirty old . . . But later on, the next day, she asked me how much. I told her it could be as much as fifty pounds if she . . . if she did what I wanted. She wouldn't, until I showed her how no one could ever recognise her."

" What have you done with the money?"

" It's in my Post Office Savings account."

" All of it?"

" I thought that perhaps one day . . ."

Bill's mind supplied the unspoken words. They struck him as the cruellest of all.

: :   : :

Bill drove slowly home and the sight of the countryside restored a little sanity to his mind.

He turned into the drive of Straightacres Farm. In the thirty-acre field, he could see a tractor ploughing up stubble. The driver was his father, doing something that gave him tremendous pleasure : midwifering a re-birth, he always called it.

Bill left his car in the garage and went into the house. His mother was in the office, working out the wages account. She looked up as he entered and when she saw the expression on his face, she drew in her breath sharply. " What's wrong, Bill?"

He shrugged his shoulders. " As far as I'm concerned, I suppose things are right. They've arrested Corinne Hammer for the murder."

" Corinne Hammer?"

" I hope I never see anything like that again." He abruptly changed the subject. " Is there enough lunch since you weren't expecting me?"

" Of course, Bill."

" I thought I'd go and see Mary this afternoon."

" I'm sure she'd like that. She was terribly upset by the trial."

"I was wondering if you could fit her in for dinner along with Joshua and his wife?"

"If you can remember to get some potted shrimps from somewhere, things will be all right. I've prepared a big meal in case either Mr. or Mrs. Tring is a big eater."

"I need a drink." He went through to the sitting-room, where he poured himself out a very strong whisky.

MAY   2006